C.O.T.C.-T]

By: Omega Kayne

THE CHRONICLES OF THE COCKSMAN

Vol. 2

©OMEGA KAYNE MEDIA 2014

Omega Kayne Media

All rights reserved. Except for use in any review, the reproduction or utilization of this work in whole or in part in any form by any electronic, mechanical, or any other means, not known or hereafter invented, including xerography, photocopying, and recording, or in any information storage or retrieval system, is forbidden without written permission of the publisher, Omega Kayne Media. For information write omegakayne@yahoo.com. All characters in this book have no existence outside of the imagination of the author and have no relation whatsoever to anyone bearing the same name or names. They are not even distantly inspired by any individual known or unknown to the author and all incidents are pure invention and coincidental.

Copyright © 2014 by Omega Kayne

ISBN-13:978-0-9891851-5-8

ISBN-10:0-9891851-5-X

Manufactured in the United States First Edition

DEDICATION

My sun shines bright because I know that it's your rays that warm my soul. It's your laughter and your energy that gives me reason to want to inspire people through words. You keep me focused because me making a better future for you is my only concern. I will utilize the gifts that JAH; THE MOST HIGH, has given to me and with everything I have, I will ensure that you are provided for. The world will know that this King has a Prince who will someday evolve into a King himself. The word "LOVE" is an understatement when I search my heart to try and convey the effect you have on me, my Prince. When I look into your big brown eyes, I fall in love again and again. You are a masterful creation and the unconditional love that you give me takes me to places that are beyond the moon. I look forward to the days ahead, when you become older; I can sit you down and tell you about all of the sacrifices that were made in order for you to be taken care of. I need you to know WHY; I did what I had to do. I want you to hear the stories of a father refusing to quit, having an unrelenting commitment to ideas. My Prince, I want you to be a trailblazer of your own path and listen to the inner voice that speaks only to you even when others are attempting to persuade you to ignore it. There's a path for you son that has not been carved out yet and as we grow older together, hopefully, my stories can be a thesis to your blueprint so that when you decide to be your own innovator my stories can be an ember to your flame.

I LOVE YOU, MY PRINCE.

Acknowledgements

To my family and friends who continue to support my efforts in sharing my gifts with the world. I appreciate you more than you know. Without word of mouth and your encouragement, my successes would not be as great so applaud you. Also, to my growing fan base……THANK YOU SO MUCH! Many of you have been with me since my early days when I began acting in the mid-90s. Now I welcome aboard a new legion of followers, KAYNEHEADS, that have joined the fast-paced KAYNE TRAIN. What would an acknowledgement be if I did not include my beautiful mother? MOM, I LOVE YOU and I THANK YOU for it ALL. I hope I'm making you PROUD. **Stephanie "Cookie" Armelin**…. You already know. THANK YOU for EVERYTHING. You are truly an ANGEL on Earth disguised as a SUPER-DUPER SISTA that is DELTA SIGMA THETA. I appreciate you, my friend, and have LOVE for you for forever and a day. And lastly Ms. Larre' Davis. You stepped right in and did a phenomenal job with this story without hesitation and I appreciate you for it. The Most High spoke and you listened.

Introduction

In "Kayne Revealed," you learned about THE MAN, THE MYTH and THE LEGEND that is Kayne. His past bred him to be the man he turned out to be and although he continued to struggle with his soul in doing so, he managed to revisit a part of his life he had been attempting to escape. Love was always a place where he wanted to seek refuge but it was tainted with inconsistencies, lies and repercussions. His heart has been torn into pieces as his affection for Olivia has brought him from the depths of disappointment to the possibility of accepting something new with Jasmine. Will Olivia come back to Kayne so that they can live the life that Kayne thinks he can have with her; or will it be riddled with costly attempts at revenge by Alexander who is not willing to give Olivia up, especially to his rival, Kayne? Will Kayne realize that what he had with Olivia was not true love at all but find it in the familiarity that lies within the Jamaican bloodline that he shares with Jasmine? One thing is for sure in this LOVE STORY: Love will be visited; Love will be tested; and Love will be lost. Who will be standing in the winner's circle in the end remains to be seen but who wallows in the loser's corner will seek the REVENGE that will rewrite "The Chronicles of the Cocksman."

Chapters of the Love Story

1. *Knock-Knock, MotherF***er*...................8
2. *Love Is All Good Until*..........................25
3. *Jasmine Wants What Jasmine Wants*..................35
4. *Games We Play*...................................53
5. *Watch Your Back*.................................61
6. *Jasmine Chronicle*...............................72
7. *The Heart Loves Who It Wants*....................85
8. *Meet the Wild Card*.............................100
9. *Olivia Has Suspicions*..........................113
10. *Meet the Congressman*..........................121
11. *Jasmine and Olivia Cross Paths*................137
12. *Millionaire Jane Chronicle*....................153
13. *He Won't Give Up On Her*.......................162
14. *He Knows*.....................................171
15. *Jasmine Makes A Stand*.........................185
16. *The Threat*...................................197
17. *Wings*..213
18. *The Decision*.................................249
19. *The Planning*.................................264
20. *That Bitch*...................................277

CHAPTER 1

<u>KNOCK...KNOCK, MOTHER****ER</u>

The door opens slowly and there he stands, looking at me as if he has just seen a ghost. He knows who I am and why I am here. At this moment you can hear the piercing sounds of hearts pounding in anticipation, they beat like two warriors drums.

"You should have never come here, Kayne. I've told you once that she's mine and that you were on borrowed time. Obviously you don't listen so I'm going to have to teach you a fucking lesson."

In the background I can see Olivia over Alexander's left shoulder with a concerned look on her face. I look at her and say, "Olivia, go get your things. You're coming with me!"

Alexander has a look of disbelief on his face, stunned that another man has come to his house to take his woman and he isn't having it. "Who do you think you are coming to my damn house disrespecting me, Kayne? I'm not having this shit! Olivia isn't going anywhere, and this is my last time telling you! You need to leave my house and never come back!"

The look on my face shows that I'm not fazed by his threats. I came for a reason. Olivia is mine and she wants to be with me. If we have to exchange blows tonight, then I came dressed for the occasion.

"Alexander, I'm walking in this house and I'm taking Olivia with me. Now you're going to move the fuck out of my way or I'm going to move you. It doesn't make a difference to me. Either way, she's coming. Now, you make the choice!"

Obviously, Alexander has had enough of the disrespect and he charges me as I walk through the door. We lock and the tussle begins. Thank goodness I decided to throw my gun in the bushes before he answered because it would have been used and I don't think that would have been a wise decision. From this point on, we engage in hand-to-hand combat. I wanted to emasculate him as much as possible, so I slapped him a few times in his fucking face to piss him off.

Olivia hears the ruckus and runs back to the living room. She looks to find us tussling on the floor, knocking over everything. Alexander is doing his best to show me that he is King and by all accounts the streets are bred in him. It's no easy task though because I'm also cut from the same cloth. We continue exchanging blows like it's a heavyweight championship fight, winner takes all.

In between blows and the rumbling I yell out to Olivia, "Get what you need and go to the car!"

That must have infuriated Alexander even more when he saw her go back to the room to get her things. At this point we are upright, shirts ripped, both heaving from the loss of breath, but neither will give in and blows continue to be thrown. Alexander keeps starring in the direction of their bedroom and sees Olivia approaching with a few bags.

While his attention is on her he forgot he was unguarded and I gave him a solid right cross that drove his ass across the room. For a moment he had to regain his wits because I landed a good one. I'm also doing my best not to show that my ribs were tender from the altercation, my adrenaline feeding my bravado.

"Kayne, I'm ready!"

Alexander is still on the floor giving Olivia a look that could cut her heart out. "If you leave this fucking house, I promise I will make every day hell for you *and* him! You will not disrespect me like this!!! You know what I'm capable of Olivia and I don't think you want those problems, do you?"

I look at Olivia as I wipe blood from my lip, "Go to the car, baby, you're coming home!" She exits the door without looking back.

"Olivia!!!!!!.......Olivia!!!!!!!!!!!"

Alexander knows he has lost the battle today but his pride won't let him accept defeat. Breathing hard and drenched in sweat, he says, "You've got a set of balls on you, Kayne. I should have known that weak bitch was going to leave me for you again. No matter how much I tried to make her forget, I knew she'd never gotten over you. Just know this, when you walk out that door you will always have to watch your back. You hear me? This is only temporary like it was before. You *will* see me again, motherfucker. She's coming back home; she always does."

From the scowl on his face I knew, from that point on, if Olivia and I were going to be together I would have to deal with his attempts to get her back. What kind of shit is this I'm getting myself into? Why do I feel that I have to have this woman? Why am I willing to put my life in jeopardy against a man who will be hell-bent on getting her back, regardless of the cost?

Obviously, I like living on the edge and a part of my ego had been fed tonight because I walked into his house, bold as shit, and took what was min! There was nothing he could do about it but sit there and watch Liv walk right out of that door.

"Alexander, face this fact, brother; she left you because she doesn't love you. It's me that she wants and it's with me that she will remain. The better man won again and you will always play second to me. Wasting your time trying to make our lives difficult will be more of a burden for you than it will be uncomfortable to me, so if you have any sense you'll take this defeat as a lesson. I'm still Kayne, motherfucker!"

I walk out of the door leaving him there with a pitiful look on his face. I walk quickly toward the car and see that Olivia is standing by the door with her bags. As I get closer, she comes to me with her arms open wide and gives me a hug that felt like forever to me. I'd missed her embrace so much and to taste her lips again felt like coming home.

"Kayne, I never want this to end. I'm so sorry for putting you through this. I promise you I will never leave you again," she said, tears streaming down her face as we kiss passionately standing in the street for all to see.

In the background I could see Alexander looking out of the curtains processing the moment that Liv and I were having. After a few minutes he just nodded his head and closed the curtains. I knew this wouldn't be the last time I'd see his face, but for now, I didn't have a care in the world. I had Olivia and she was coming home where she belonged.

Driving home, my phone rings. I picked it up and noticed it was Jasmine calling again. I look over and see that Olivia has fallen asleep and didn't hear the phone ring, or so I thought, but I declined the call and switched it to vibrate just in case Jasmine decided to call again.

Everything seemed to be in slow motion. It seemed like forever for us to arrive home. When I pulled up to my place, Olivia awoke and smiled confidently, as if she knew that everything was going to be all right.

She reached over and grabbed my hand, kissed me and said, "Why didn't you answer your phone, Kayne? Who was that, baby?"

Like I said, I thought she was asleep and now I have to begin our reunion with a lie. There's no way I can tell her about Jasmine; not now, not ever.

So, I looked at her and said, "It came up as an 'unknown' caller and I don't answer those calls."

She smiles and says, "OK, Kayne," and we head into the house.

Once we get upstairs, Olivia walks in and just stands in the middle of the foyer and stares in silence surveying the place.

"What's wrong, baby?"

She doesn't respond. She closes her eyes, takes in three deep breaths, turns to me and says, "I'm free, Kayne. I can breathe here. I'm where I'm supposed to be," and she drops to her knees and begins to cry uncontrollably.

I put my arms around her and pull her close to me, letting her have her moment. Truth is, I was crying, too because a part of my heart that had been snatched away was now being mended because 'my heart' was lying in my arms. It seemed like she lay in my arms for hours, weeping and continuously apologizing for leaving in the first place.

"Liv, why did you leave me like that? I thought we had something."

She looked up at me, wiped her face and said, "I had to, Kayne. I couldn't stay. You don't know what Alexander is capable of."

"What do you mean?"

She sits upright now as the tone of our conversation is getting more serious. "Alexander feels that he owns me. Years ago, I was in this bad relationship before I met him and he pretty much saved me from it. I was homeless. I had no money, no job, nowhere to go and he took me in. I didn't like him initially, but grew to eventually love him because I had nowhere else to go."

Still taking in her story, I managed to ask, "So you stayed with him out of necessity?"

With a look of embarrassment on her face, she replied, "Yes. I needed help and he was there to provide it. The days turned into years and every time I tried to leave him, he would threaten to hurt me."

Now, this was sort of making sense to me; why she'd just left me high and dry.

"So you were trying not to get me involved?"

"Exactly, I knew if I stayed with you, and away from him, he wouldn't stop until he found me and I care for you too much to bring you into my mess."

I'm realizing now that there is so much more I need to know about Olivia and some questions need to be answered.

"Baby, you could have handled this differently. You had me worried…No, you had my mind fucked up and I don't like that. I love you, Olivia, and I want you to be with me. So, I'm asking you now, can you please just be honest with me from this point on?"

She pauses for a quick moment and grabs my face, "I will. I promise."

She had the most sincere look on her face and I somewhat felt comfortable with the response, but part of me will not believe her just yet because when she left me the first time my trust was broken and I knew that bridge was going to be hard to rebuild.

Still interested in getting information, I began to pry a little. "Olivia, I never asked you this before, but what's your story? I mean, we just fell into each other's arms and never really revealed that much about ourselves. So, let's start all over again. Is that cool?"

Without hesitation, she nods her head and says, "Cool."

Still sitting on the floor we begin to talk like we had just met. "Ok, Kayne. You want to know about Olivia, so here we go. I was born and raised here in Los Angeles and I'm an only child. I grew up in a very strict household and wasn't allowed to do much of anything. My parents kept a tight rein on me, especially my father, who later caused me to resent him and I became a rebellious soul."

"Where are your parents now?" I asked.

"Well my father passed away a few years ago and I haven't seen my mother in years. After my dad passed, I left home for good because I just needed to be away. While I was there it seemed like I was in prison and my mother never challenged my father on anything. She never took up for me even when I was right and I've never really forgiven her for that."

Taking all of this information in, I ask, "So was this around the time that you were in the bad relationship that you spoke of?"

"Yes. That's when I met Jason. He was someone I was familiar with and at the time he made me feel like I was the most beautiful girl in the world and that I didn't need to be held captive. At first, he made feel like a princess, but then he became possessive and it was just like it was when I was growing up with my parents. Many times I tried to leave him but he would always find me and force me back."

It's unbelievable to me that someone so beautiful could have so much turmoil in her life, all because of her choices. "So what was the last straw?"

She looks at me with a hurt look on her face and I knew what was about to come out of her mouth was going to be just as painful as what she has already revealed. "I lost my baby because of him. He beat me so bad once that I miscarried and, afterwards, he looked me in my face and said that it was what I deserved for running away."

I have always felt that a man who has to put his hands on a woman is not a man and his insecurities run deeper than the average. I have no sympathy for those types and to beat a pregnant woman is inexcusable. Deep down, I truly felt sorry for Olivia because, although her beauty is unbelievable, you can also see a story untold in her eyes and tonight she is revealing that story to me. And, as much as her pain hurts me right now, I continue to listen.

"Kayne, that ripped my heart out. I wanted to be a mother. I wanted a child and he took that away from me. After that, I ran away for good and lived on the streets until I met Alexander."

"How did you and Alexander meet?"

She takes a deep breath, as if to say, 'I hope you're prepared to hear this,' and says, "When I left Jason, I had no place to go. I had no money, so I had to do what I had to do." Still listening, I give her a 'please continue' look.

"I worked the streets, Kayne. Alexander was a John of mine. One time became ten, and eventually, he just took me in."

Now this was a 'wow' moment for me. Here I am, concerned about revealing my lifestyle to her for fear of being judged, and she has a story, too…and it's ok. Everyone has a road that they have taken to get where they are today. No matter the vehicle used to get there, you still had to get there, and I was in no position to see her any differently than I had before she revealed her story.

"I know that's something you weren't prepared to hear, Kayne, but it's my truth. I had to survive because I had no other skills at the time. It was by luck that I got that job at the hotel where I met you."

"Whatever happened to Jason?"

She gives me the same look she'd just given me, so I know the answer to this was going to be just as revealing. "Alexander made him go away. I never saw him again."

Now, a concerned look comes over my face because that could mean one or two things, so I look for clarification. "What do you mean, *he made him go away?*"

"You know what I mean, Kayne. Alexander personally made him go away and, this is why I had to leave you when I did. I know what he's capable of."

Taking in all she has just said, all I could do was take a deep breath because now it's been confirmed. My days from this point on with Olivia will be filled with drama. Why am I choosing to accept that? Why am I willing to put myself in harm's way for this woman? Why am I so drawn to her? Is it that her story is familiar to me and I can understand her fight? Right now, I don't know, but I'm sure more answers will come with time.

We must have sat on the floor and exchanged stories for hours and I'm glad we did because we both learned some things about each other that we never knew. After the conversation we both took a shower and cleansed the drama of the day off. Afterward, we lay in bed staring at the ceiling and, just like that, the old feelings came back like they had never left us. I could feel her body starting to warm just by lying next to me and I was beginning to feel my blood flow to that place where the legend was made. He started to move like he knew who I was with and he knew exactly where he wanted to go.

Olivia began to rub on him really slow while massaging my full length and it felt good. She knew exactly what I liked and she wasted no time letting me know her memory wasn't at a loss. She took her warm mouth and placed my hard muscle in it very slowly. She made sure she paid close attention to every inch of me and used her tongue like a magic wand. I'd missed the way she would take me there and make me feel so GOOD. As I'm looking at her go to work, covering the evidence of my manhood with all of her saliva she manages to get in a few words.

"Did you miss this, baby? You wanted this, Kayne?"

You damn right I'd missed it and I wanted it and as always, she served me up right! She made a figure-eight with her tongue as she sucked and licked my tool and all around my balls. Fuck!!! This was what I'd missed, what I needed and I couldn't wait to get inside of her and taste her honey.

I whisper in her ear, "Let me taste you now, baby."

It must have been music to her ears because she wasted no time in opening her legs, putting her hands underneath her knees and holding her thighs wide open. I can tell she hadn't shaved in some days and hair was everywhere. SHE KNOWS I LOVE THAT SHIT, and when I saw that, I knew I was going to fill her up to capacity.

I take my middle and index fingers and open her glistening lips. I place my warm mouth over the entrance of her most prized possession. Slowly, I suck on her opening and stick my tongue deep inside her. Her moans were like she had never felt this before. She grabbed the back of my head and forced every inch of my hot tongue inside of her…and I didn't mind. I placed my lips tightly and strategically over her swollen clit and flicked my tongue over it really quickly, driving her crazy.

"Oh, shit, Kayne! Oh, fuck! Right there, baby, right fucking there!"

She remembered now how good I was with my mouth and I didn't stop. She came quickly and once again within the first fifteen minutes of me indulging. Her nectar was still sweet to the taste and I swallowed all of it.

I cuffed my mouth over her water flow with my tongue still strong inside of her walls and drank all of her release.

She sat up in the bed, panting heavily and said, 'Now fuck me from the back!" and quickly got on all fours and reaching back to spread her cheeks.

My view was a hairy hole covered with wet saliva mixed with her cream. I quickly put on the gold packet. Instinctively, he knew where to go and what to do so I helped him find his direction and inserted him where he is always happy.

"Ahhhhhhhhhhhhhhhhh!"

She let out a long moan as if she was relieved by the heat of my manhood. I grabbed her hips and began to thrust inside her at a rapid pace. She didn't want slow love making. She wanted that fire because her eyes told me so.

Just then, she turns back and looks at me while I'm doing my best to pull out more orgasms and says, 'This is what I'm talking about. This dick is so fucking good Kayne! Oh, my god! I don't want you giving this to nobody else but me! Promise me, Kayne…promise me!"

Caught up in the moment, I said I wouldn't; but I knew that I may have told an untruth because, even in the throes of passion with Olivia, Jasmine was still in the back of my mind. Of course, I didn't disclose that fact. I just kept pounding away until both of our bodies were covered with sweat.

A handful of orgasms and several hours later, we lay in bed asleep, holding each other like only today mattered, and began our life all over again. I'm sure we will soon be faced with some type of adversity, especially after learning more of Alexander's background and what he is capable of. His obsession with Olivia will definitely be a problem, so I know I'll have to be ready for any bullshit that may come my way.

As for Jasmine, I don't know how I'm going to handle that situation, but I'm drawn to her and I want to know if what we felt in Jamaica was real. Again, I'm starting out being dishonest but it's that trust thing that I've always fought and will continue to fight until I believe in it again. So, I'll flow as I go. It's Kayne and Olivia…for now.

CHAPTER 2

LOVE IS ALL GOOD UNTIL...

Weeks have gone by and Olivia and I are living in total bliss. It's like we'd never parted, acting as though forever really exists. I had not been on the clock for a while as I was trying to deal with my emotional dilemma but the life is calling me. I had a big nest egg saved up but I knew that it would lose its girth pretty soon. I need to make sure money is always flowing, so there is a strong possibility that I may need to revisit the life.

    Olivia had to quit her job at the hotel because Alexander had been calling and making threats, so I told her to let it go, we would be fine. I don't know how she would feel about me taking on clients again but we needed to have that conversation before I indulged. I don't plan on lying to her if I don't have to. This woman has brought about feelings in me that I thought were dead. She treats me like a King and I don't want it to end so, if it's within me, I'm going to continue to do the things that warrant that treatment. Let's just hope she's ok with THE COCKSMAN being the Cocksman. This is just business as always.

It's the middle of the afternoon and Olivia has been cleaning house and giving it a woman's touch. "Baby, this place doesn't look like a bachelor's pad anymore."

She smiles and replies, "You aren't a bachelor. You have a woman and this is a reflection of your life now. The Cocksman days are over for you buddy."

Well, I guess I have the answer to what I was going to discuss with her. Obviously, she is speaking from emotion right now. I'm her man and she doesn't want to share but, hell, we got to eat and pay bills. She isn't working, so there's no better time than the present to bring it up. "Liv, I want to talk to you about that."

She gives me a concerned look and says, "Talk to me about what?"

Here we go. "Baby, I may have to get back on the clock. Money is getting low."

I could see a myriad of emotions set on her face as I expected the response I was about to receive. "Oh, no, the fuck you won't! That will not be happening, Kayne! You better go back to the corporate world! Your dick-slinging days are over!" And, she storms out of the room.

Shaking my head because I knew it would go down like this, I go to the bedroom to continue the conversation.

"Olivia, I understand that you may feel a certain kind of way about how I made my living, but look around you and you tell me what kind of job can you get to help support this lifestyle?" There's a long pause because she knows her ass isn't qualified to answer the question.

"I don't want to talk about this anymore. I don't care about what we have. We can downsize, Kayne."

Ok, I'm trying to remain calm about this but now she's bringing me to a place called reality and I'm about to bring her ass with me. "No. We are not downsizing anything that I've earned. Quick question, are you working now?" No response.

"Can you afford to pay for this on your own?" Still, there's no damn response.

"I saw where you were living with Alexander. Do you want to go back to that lifestyle?" She just sits there in silence.

"Listen, baby, I understand, really, I do. But how are we supposed to maintain? I'm not interested in going back into that hamster-on-a-wheel machine called Corporate America and you definitely don't have a skill that could make the kind of money we need to take care of us."

That comment must have pissed her off because she sat up and responded, "What the hell do you mean I don't have a skill to make money, Kayne! I have the same skill that the Cocksman does! How would you like that?"

I would love to agree with her because she definitely has some skills but there's no way in hell that I would agree to her doing what I do. "That's definitely not going to happen so get that out of your mind. As a matter of fact, don't you ever mention that to me again."

Now, the myriad of emotions on her face has turned into a smirk, "Oh, have I touched a sore spot, Kayne? What? You can't imagine another man getting some of this sweet, brown wet? You don't like the thought of that do you?"

Of course I don't want to imagine anyone else but me inside of Olivia, but if I gave her the answer she's expecting, I wouldn't have a leg to stand on. "It's not the same thing Olivia…period," and I walk out to the living room to watch TV.

This conversation didn't go well at all and neither one of us got the response we expected. Do I go behind her back and live the Cocksman lifestyle or do I go back to the corporate world where my earning power has a ceiling?

There is no way in hell that I will go back to a life where someone else controls my elevation, so this will have to be the first lie I tell and the first secret I keep from Olivia since our fresh start. She doesn't know how much money I have saved and I'll never tell her. I'll have to find a way to strategically work my flow so she wouldn't have a clue as to what I'm doing. I just need one big hit, one client that I can keep on retainer and I know she's out there. I need to open up my network and get my name back out to take over the market again.

My mind is racing with ideas and new ways to get back on my grind, and then my cell phone rings. I look at the screen and its Jasmine calling again. I've ignored her calls before and I can't do it again; but, do I take the chance on getting caught by Olivia who's right in the next room? It's now on its third ring and my debate is real. I go into the kitchen and answer it, making sure my voice is low enough where only I can hear it.

"Hello, Jasmine. How are you?"

In the sweetest patois accent, she responds, "So, yuh finally answer my call! Meh gwan have to find yuh when I come dere in two days."

I know I didn't just hear what I think I heard. I want to see her bad but my current situation will definitely complicate things. How do I respond to this woman without making her feel like I'm blowing her off? Should I try a different approach by changing the subject?

"So, how have you been, Jasmine? It's been a while since we've spoken. How is work? Are you doing a lot of travelling?"

There was a short pause and a deep breath before she responded, and this time there was not one trace of patois. "Kayne, did you hear me? I said I'm coming to Los Angeles in two days and I was hoping that I could see you."

Fuck me!!!!! This is the worst timing in the world, but I can't turn her away this time. I'm going to have to find a way to see her and spend time without letting Olivia know what's on my agenda.

"I heard you Jasmine. I was just so excited to hear your voice that I wanted to catch up with you to see how things have been going since last we spoke."

"Well, we can catch up when I get there. I'll be staying at the Chateau Marmont for a couple of days on business and then I'll be in town for a few more days. I was hoping that I could come and stay with you if that's OK?"

Are you kidding me? This is not my life right now. What am I supposed to say to that? I can't say yes, knowing damn well that Olivia is here at my place. Jasmine has no idea about my situation and I know I should tell her, but dammit I want her…BAD. I want my dream of her to be a reality soon. Here I go again digging myself into an emotional hole that I know will be too deep for me to climb out of but fuck it. You only live once, right?

"Sure, you can stay for as long as you like." How I'm going to pull this off is beyond me, but I had to keep this charade up until I could figure out a contingency plan.

"Good. I was hoping that you'd say yes. I really want to spend some quality time with you, Kayne, and I have to admit that my quality time will include any and everything because I've been thinking about you a lot since we met. I felt our connection back on the island and I know you know what I mean. I'm curious too about all of you and hopefully we can share our own little universe and exchange energy."

My curiosity piques, I say, "Really? Tell me more."

Suddenly, I hear the bedroom door open and Olivia calls out my name, "Kayne!"

I quickly hang up the phone before Jasmine can respond. I turn my phone off and go back to the living room to meet Olivia. She's giving me a very suspicious look, like my cat was out of the bag.

"Why were you in the kitchen talking on the phone?"

I'm trying to come up with a quick answer because, obviously, I don't have one and I respond, "What are you talking about?" Yeah, this was the best I could think of on the fly.

"I'm saying this one more time, Kayne. I hope you're not hiding anything from me. You said you would be totally honest with me. It would not be a good thing if I found out that you're lying to me. We promised each other that we wouldn't do that. No more secrets, right?"

Now, this is the moment that I can tell her about my decision to go back on the clock and about Jasmine but, again, I fail to do so. "There's nothing to tell, Liv. Why are you tripping?" I head to the bedroom to kill the vibe but she quickly follows me.

"I'm just getting a feeling and it's not a good one."

Still attempting to deflect, I say, "I think you're overreacting, Olivia. Everything's fine and I have nothing to hide from you."

I'm hoping she doesn't smell the lies that were oozing from my pores because I sure could, but there was no way in hell that I was going to reveal anything now. It was too soon and we just got back on track.

Rooted to one spot, Olivia stared wordlessly at me. It was like she was giving me a chance to come clean, but I choose not to. "What? Say something."

Still nothing comes out. Just that damn look that's eating through my lying armor. I have to focus on lightening the moment and taking her mind off her suspicions. "Hey, we need to go shopping. We're almost out of food."

Still looking at me she gives a coy smile while shaking her head, "I'll go. I want to get out of the house for a while anyway. I need money and the keys," and walks away to get her purse.

I knew this wasn't over by the look on her face. It's funny how she can be so suspicious of me and it was her ass that left me. She was the one who neglected to tell me she sold ass for a living. At least she knew up front what my hustle was. It's whatever. This too shall pass.

I give her two hundred dollars and my keys then I go back to the living room to watch television. She walks out the door without saying anything. I signed up for this but who can blame her for being suspicious? A woman knows when something is wrong and when things are different just like a man, but I'm going to do my best to fight the urge to be honest and hide what I know will change our rekindled relationship. So, for now, I've got to keep *"Project Jasmine"* on the low and *"Project on the Clock"* well-hidden.

CHAPTER 3

JASMINE WANTS WHAT JASMINE WANTS

The last couple of days have been really tense between Liv and me. She's been acting very calm, a bit too calm for me but I decided not to ruffle her feathers. I'm going to follow her lead but I know that there's a storm brewing just beneath the surface of her outward calmness. She's reminding me of a lioness who sits and waits for something to disrupt her den so she can make felt the full power of ferocious growl. So far, I have never heard Olivia's growl. I don't even know if she has one and I'm not sure I want to find out.

As I'm dealing with the tension at home, I'm also feeling the anticipation of Jasmine's arrival. I still don't have a clue how I'm going to pull this off but there's no way in hell that she'll be able to come to my house.

As I'm sitting on the couch flipping through channels, Olivia is going back and forth from the bedroom to the kitchen doing various things and keeping busy. I try to strike up a conversation, "Babe, what's happening? You haven't been still all day."

She continues to make her way around the house, not giving a response. I know there's something on her mind and I may as well break this awkward silence and face whatever she is thinking so I get up and stand in her path.

"Olivia, what the hell is going on with you?"

Before she could give me an answer, my cell rings. Oh, shit! I really do have the worst luck. I'm hoping that this isn't who I think it is. I'm looking at Olivia as if I'm still waiting on her to answer me but she isn't buying into it. "Aren't you are going to answer your phone?"

I stand there motionless, not answering her question or the ringing phone. Jasmine had said she would be in town today and that she would call me. Not now, not at this fucking moment.

"Kayne, why won't you answer your damn phone? Fuck this! I'm going to answer it," and moves toward the counter where the phone lay.

I quickly follow behind her and we get to the phone at the same time. The shit is about to hit the fan once she sees Jasmine's name on that screen. My spot is about to be blown up. She picks up the phone and gets a look at the screen as it showed………. *"Mom"* calling.

You could have heard my heart drop out of my damn chest and hit the floor but I was so glad it wasn't

Jasmine calling. Olivia hands me the phone and shakes her head. She could tell I was vexed but I still played it as cool as I could considering what I thought what was about to happen.

"Hello, Mom. How are you doing?"

She gives me a short pause before she answers. There was no *patois* in her response and I found that quite peculiar as she always speaks to me in her native accent.

"I'm OK, son. You were just on my mind and I wanted to hear your voice." I could tell by her demeanor on the phone something wasn't right so I pressed a bit.

"I'm doing well, Mom, but how are you? You sound different. Is something wrong?"

Her next response was just as uncanny as her initial one. "So, when will I see my son again? When will you come visit me?"

This is so not like my mom, and Olivia could see that I was bothered as she mouthed, "*Is your mom OK?*" All I could do was shrug my shoulders as if to say, "*I don't know,*" and walk toward the bedroom to continue the conversation.

"Mom, I don't know when I'm coming to visit but I will definitely come soon if you want me to."

I notice that she keeps coughing on the other end of the phone. "(COUGH! COUGH! COUGH!)That would be nice, son, real nice."

Concerned, I ask, "Do you have a cold?"

She tries to lighten the mood by laughing. "Meh hav a bit of cough son. Yah Muddah gwan bey fine. But, that's enough about me. Wha beh gwan on wit you? Meh nuh heard from yuh?"

Of course, there's plenty that I could say, but why burden her with my ever-growing list of problems? Plus, knowing my mother, she already has a feeling that one of the reasons why I haven't called her in a while is because I am navigating through my own issues.

"Everything has been cool…nothing really to talk about mom. I'm just living my life out here in Cali."

I swear that sometimes my mother and I can read each other's minds because I knew her next question before she uttered a word.

"So, is my son getting married anytime soon? Whatever happened to the girl that you were so in love with?"

I could see Olivia sitting on the couch from where I stood. "Olivia, Mom…her name is Olivia. Well, we worked it all out and we're back together."

Her coughing is more noticeable as she struggles to get her words out. "Well good for you. Hopefully, I'll get to meet this young lady before it's too late."

I didn't understand what she meant by "too late," and as I was about to ask what she meant by it, I see that Jasmine is calling in. I tell my mom to hold for a second and answer the call, making sure that Olivia is still in the living room.

"Hello, Jasmine. Are you here?"

She seemed surprised that I answered and laughed, "Oh, my! Kayne answered the phone. This must be my lucky day. Yes, I am in the City of Angels. I want to see you, Kayne. Are you free?"

Shit is about to get real! I get up to check on Olivia and see that she's getting up, so I quickly go to the corner of the bedroom and respond, "Of course, I'm free, but I'm on the other line with my mom. Text me the address of your hotel and your room number and I'll be there in a few hours, OK?"

By this time, Olivia has made it to the bedroom. I quickly hang up on Jasmine without even saying goodbye and click back over to my mom.

"Mom…Mom are you there?" I hadn't heard her hang up on the other end but she was gone.

"Is your mom OK, Kayne?"

I tell you, I'm surviving by the skin of my teeth, trying to juggle these two women but I remain calm and answer, "Yes, she just misses me and asked when I will come and see her."

Jumping on that statement, Olivia quickly asks, "So, when are we going so I can meet your mom?"

"As soon as I can make time to get down there, but right now I need to go wire her some money. That's why she was calling."

Yes, that was just a lie to get out of the house so I could go and meet up with Jasmine. The closest Western Union was at least half an hour away and traffic was bad at this time of the day, so I knew it would buy me some time.

But, just as I grab my keys, Olivia grabs her shoes and says, "I'll come with you. I need to get out of this house for a little while, too."

Ain't this about a bitch?!? I scramble to think of something to throw her off without it seeming like I really don't want her to come with me.

"Babe, I thought you were going to cook tonight. You took those steaks out and I was really looking forward to it. I won't be long. Why don't you stay here and get dinner started? When I get back we can eat and watch a movie."

To my relief, she put her shoes back down and agreed. "Yeah, I forgot I took those steaks out to cook tonight. Dinner will be ready when you get back. Hurry back…and don't forget how to get home, Kayne," and walks to the kitchen to start cooking.

As I head for the door, the text comes through from Jasmine. I take a look at it to memorize the information and quickly delete it before I leave because sometimes I forget to keep my phone on automatic lock.

While driving in this god awful L.A. traffic, my mind takes me back to when I was home in Jamaica with Jasmine and the dream I had about her. It still seemed too real, like it was meant to happen, and as much as I want to be faithful to Olivia, I also want to know what Jasmine smells, feels and tastes like. Of course, I'm not going to immediately hit her with those expectations, but I know I won't turn it down if it's offered. In any case, I'm going to take some of these condoms that I have hidden in my car with me.

I pull up to the hotel and text her, "*I'm here and I'm coming up now.*"

She replies, "*I'm in the lobby at the bar. See you when you get here.*"

I haven't had butterflies since I was a kid, but they are definitely stirring in my stomach right now. I didn't even have these when I first met Olivia. Jasmine just gives me a different feeling. She's a different kind of woman. There is a class about her that makes me feel like I have to know more about her and now that she's here in my city, there's no turning back.

As I walk in the door, the doorman nods and welcomes me in. I see that the bar is off to the left side of the lobby. There are a good amount of people sitting around, drinking and having conversation. As I get closer to the bar, I see her and damn, this woman is looking good! She notices me and gives me a big smile. She has on a black Bodycon dress by Alexander McQueen with four-inch Walter Steiger stilettos, gold bottoms that propped her ass up like a perfect apple.

As I got closer, she stood to give me a hug. She smelled magnificent and when she pressed her body against mine, I took in her every angle and every curve. Her breasts melted into my chest as I wrapped my arms around her tiny waist, clinching my hands together to hold her even tighter. She soon broke contact to look into my eyes and I knew at that moment, I was hooked again.

Sighing, she says, "I've missed you, Kayne," and gives me a kiss right there in the middle of the crowded bar. If she didn't mind, then I didn't either, and returned her kiss as I caressed her waistline.

"So you really missed me, huh?" as we both laughed and took a seat.

We sat at the bar for hours, laughing and talking. It was as if no one else was there; the only conversation taking place was ours. It was so good to see Jasmine again. I knew that being this close to her was rekindling the feelings I'd developed for her in Jamaica. But, as good as it felt to be with Jasmine, I have to get back home. Olivia is waiting and I'm surprised that she hasn't called to see what was taking so long.

I could see that Jasmine had gotten a bit tipsy after several glasses of wine. She had a look in her eyes that told me we could have that night I had once dreamt about.

"Kayne, what are your plans for the rest of the evening?"

I know the answer I want to give her, but I have to be smarter than that. I know I'm in for one hell of an argument when I get home tonight, and the longer I stay here, the worse it will be.

"Well, I know you have to work tomorrow so I'm about to go so you can get some rest. I have a few things to do when I get home anyway.

Jasmine stands and grabs my hand. "You don't have to leave. You can stay with me tonight and leave in the morning. I'm well-rested."

No! No! No!!! In my mind I'm screaming because that's exactly what I want to do but can't; so I try and remain calm and give her a coy reply, "Are you sure you want that, Jasmine? Trust me; you may not be ready for that."

She gives me a look that challenges what I'd just said. She takes out an extra key card, pushes it towards me and begins to walk away. "When you're ready, I'm in Suite #702."

She gives me that sweet, sexy ass smile again before she gets in the elevator and just like a bad-ending movie, my phone rings. It's Olivia. Should I send this call to voicemail and deal with the ramifications when I get home, or answer it and hear her mouth? Fuck it, I'll answer and deal with the tirade. "Hello."

There is a very long pause before she responds, so I know she's pissed. "Kayne, where are you? It doesn't take two damn hours to get to a Western Union!"

Knowing how bad traffic can be in Los Angeles, that's the excuse I use. "Baby, I'm still in traffic but I'm on the way back now. You know how this traffic is," covering the phone to hide the background noise.

"So you're driving home now? What's the noise in the background, Kayne?" Shit! I better think quickly!

I get an incoming call and see it's from Jasmine, so I say to Liv, "Hey, babe. This is my mom. I'm sure she's calling about the money, Let me take this call and I'll call you back, ok?" and quickly click over before she can respond. I know I'll pay for that later, but I switch over to take Jasmine's call anyway.

"Jasmine!"

"Are you coming, Kayne? I'm waiting for you."

Quickly, I respond, "I'm on my way now."

Now, as I'm walking toward the elevator, I'm having flashbacks to my time in Jamaica when Jasmine and I met and that damn dream. Will this be the night I get to taste the inner patois between Jasmine's legs? Will I be able to feel how warm her pussy is as I slowly stroke her insides with my thick, West Indian stick? Am I about to hear her moan as I put every inch of my manhood inside of her and watch her eyes roll in the back of her head?

The elevator door opens and I head to Suite 702. My dick must know where I'm going and what's to come because he's already thick and throbbing. I need to get into her wet hole now and as I get closer to her room, my dick is growing longer.

I swipe the key in and open the door. The lights are already out and there is music playing. I can hear that Jasmine is in the shower so I call out to her. "Jasmine, I'm here."

She hears me and responds, "OK. Make yourself comfortable, baby. I'll be out in a few." If this is about to go down like I'm thinking it will, I want to go and get in the shower with her.

Dammit! My phone rings again and it's Olivia. I walk over toward the living area and take the call before Jasmine gets out of the shower. Lowering my voice, I say, "What's up, Olivia?"

Not wasting anytime, she gives me a piece of her mind. "Are you still on the phone with your mother, Kayne? Why in the hell did you hang up on me? You are acting really strange. What in the fuck is going on?!" From her tone, I can tell that nothing I say will matter because Olivia is already heated, so I remain silent.

Just then, I hear the shower stop. Jasmine is about to open the door and walk out of the bathroom, so I pretend I'm having a bad connection.

"Liv, can you hear me?..... Liv!!!"

Obviously Olivia is much smarter than that because she responds, "If you hang up this fucking phone on me pretending you have a bad connection, you may as well stay your ass out for the night!"

Whether she believed me or not, I'm still going along with my idea. "Liv, I can't hear you, baby. I'll call you back," and hung up the phone just as Jasmine walks out of the bathroom in a full body suit of black lace that's hugging every curve on her salacious body. She has that hungry look in her eyes but I'm remaining calm until she crosses the sexual *come fuck me* line that I have drawn in the imaginary sand. Then I'll take her ass right where she stands.

"Let me put on a robe."

A robe? "Why does she need to put on a robe," I ask myself. Obviously, she knows exactly what she's doing and my muscle knows too because he's trying to unzip my pants himself to get to her.

"Why the robe Jasmine? I mean, it's not really needed, you know," I say, sarcastically.

She responds, "Well, I don't want to put you in a situation that may compromise your decision to leave. I know you have important things to do, so I think I better cover up," and bends over to pick up the robe that's lying across the ottoman. "Maybe when I come over to your house in a couple of days I won't need this robe."

From my angle, I can see the tightness of that body suit splitting her swollen nether lips. This woman is teasing me purposely but I love it. As she ties the robe around her waist I stand there hard as a fucking rock. I see her eyes go down to where my thickness is calling her and she just smiles. She knows I want her and I'm wondering if tonight will be the night I can have her.

It's almost midnight now and my phone has been silent since my last conversation with Olivia. Jasmine and I have moved our conversation to the bed.

She looks at me with those mesmerizing eyes and says, "Tonight has been quite wonderful, Kayne. Our conversation was pleasant and it's no secret that there is a strong attraction between us. I know you said you had to leave but I would like it if you would stay the night with me," then she grabs my face and gives me a long, warm, wet kiss.

I know if I stay, it's going to go down. I also know that my house will be a hurricane if I show up when the sun rises, but this woman is tempting me something awful.

"So, will you? Please don't tell me I have to beg you to spend the night with all of this," then, she lies on her back and props her feet up on the bed, legs wide open rubbing on her full breasts.

I just may have to deal with the consequences because I have to have this woman; but, just when I'm about to put my hands in her heated furnace, my cell rings. I already know who it is. Thank goodness I put it on vibrate, but still Jasmine asked, "Aren't you going to answer it? Someone calling this time of night, it may be an emergency."

I look at the screen just to confirm that it's my "supervisor," Olivia. Damn! This night will have to be continued. A big part of me wanted to say, "*Fuck it*" and stay, but my heart said, "*Go home now!*"

Thinking quickly, I say, "It's a colleague from the east coast who I'm doing a project with. This is why I have to leave. I better get going, Jasmine." Then, I get up and head to the door.

Jasmine gets up and follows me and, as I stand at the open door ready to leave, she gives me a tight hug and another kiss and says, "Imagine what tonight could have been," as she rubs the visible imprint of my manhood that is now aching to get loose. "I'll see you in a couple of days,

Kayne. I'm looking forward to coming to your home so we can give him some relief."

She is indeed a beast and she's calling to the beast inside me, but Olivia won this round tonight because I'm trying to do right. I mean, I did go and take her away from that punk bitch, Alexander. I did leave Jamaica early to come and save her, so why am I here?

I know why. It's because I am who I am and I'm a glutton for punishment. My chronicle with Jasmine will have to wait for now because I still have to figure out how I'm going to pull off juggling these two women, and most of all, I have to get ready for the drama I'm going to have to deal with when I get home tonight.

Speeding on the highway and still hard from my rendezvous with Jasmine, I had to pull him out and relieve him of his agony. I stroked him and rubbed him and, as I reach one hundred miles per hour, he released the biggest wad of cream right there within the confines of my BMW 7-series.

I pull up to my home. I just sit there for a while cleaning myself off and anticipating the fight I'm going to have with Olivia when I get upstairs. I love Olivia; I really do, but Jasmine is going to make it hard for me to remain on the straight and narrow. I've already started off on the wrong foot with these lies and I'm really tripping. The heart loves who it loves, until it sees something it really wants, and right now, the heart that loves Olivia *really wants Jasmine.*

    In the house I go...

CHAPTER 4

GAMES WE PLAY

I couldn't get into the house fast enough before Olivia met me at the door. "Where were you Kayne, why did it take you so damn long to come back?" I didn't expect her to be up much less meeting me at the damn door and I just said the first thing that came to my mind. "Well after I was stuck in traffic, I just sat in my car and listened to music downstairs to clear my mind."

You could hear her anger building up and she was furious and then out of nowhere, she slaps me in the face.

"You are a fucking liar, I know that's not the truth, as a matter of fact let me see the Western Union receipt from sending your mom the money?!" God knows I don't have a receipt to show this woman and my lies keep digging a deeper hole that is going to be much harder to pull myself out but I find myself having to do so to save the feelings that I know are fragile. I'm doing a horrible job as I continue to see how deep of a hole I can dig.

"I never keep those things Olivia, I threw it away in the store" and I walked toward the bathroom to take a shower. Like a heat seeking missile, Liv followed fast still yelling and attempting to hear more of my inexcusable answers. "Kayne, I can't believe that you are straight up lying to me. You claim that you needed and wanted me back in your life and this is how you treat me? You didn't go and do what you said you were going to do and you better believe I'm going to find out what is going on," as she storms out of the room leaving me there wondering what does she mean she is going to find out?

I'm hoping after a good night's sleep some of this suspiciousness that I've caused can wear off a little and I can talk to her. Quite honestly I had never seen her this mad before and the look in her eyes meant something deeper than me just lying and her knowing it.

That look she gave me was a look of "*You continue to do me this way and you will get exactly what is meant for you*" look.

Do I believe she will find out what I'm trying to hide from her? Well if it's up to me, she won't and I'll do everything to keep her away from the truth. Since Olivia decided not to sleep in the room tonight I figured we'd both get some peaceful rest and deal with each other tomorrow.

It's almost four in the morning and Olivia hasn't made it to bed yet so I get up to go out and check on her in the living room because I'd rather have her be in bed with me and I felt like I needed to shed some truth to her so I head to the living room where I thought I'd find her on the couch but there was no sign of her.

I go to the loft to check but Olivia was nowhere to be found. "Olivia!" and the room is silent with no response. I see that my keys were not in the usual spot so I look around the house and bathrooms just in case she is there and still nothing. I look outside and notice that my fucking car is gone.

Olivia has taken my car and left at four in the morning so I grab my cell and call her immediately as all kinds of thoughts began to cross my mind. Where is she? Did she go back to Alexander? Is she Ok? Is my car ok? I dial her number and it quickly goes to voicemail. This shit can't be happening? I must have called her phone 20 times in just as many minutes and I get no response from her. I go and put on some clothes and I walk outside and sit on the steps to think and wait.

It is close to 5 in the morning and there are still no signs on Olivia anywhere so I go back inside and look for anything that may be able to tell me something. I've noticed that an overnight bag that she always uses is gone from the closet. I'm getting hot now because I know this bitch hasn't taken my car to go and see another man. My mind tells me to call over to Alexander's house right now to see if she was there but I'm refusing that thought with all of my might.

She wouldn't dare go back to him or would she? Is she trying to get me jealous or give me a taste of my own medicine? After hours of waiting, I must have fallen asleep on the couch and I was awakened by her keying in. I look over at the clock and notice that it is now 8:45 in the morning. She didn't try to sneak in at all, she made as much noise as keying in and slamming the door would allow like she wanted me to know that she was just getting in.

She sees me lying on the couch but she walks right past me without saying a word. "Olivia, why did you take my car and leave here that time of night? Where did you go?" She just looks at me and keeps walking toward the bathroom. Before she could close it I stop it with my hands and she begins to get undressed to get in the shower.

Now I'm perplexed as I need to know now where she has been and why she needs to take a goddamn shower. "Why are you taking a shower Olivia? Where have you been? Did you go see Alexander?!" And that must have gotten her attention because she gave me that look again and a smirk like she knew that whatever her answer would be it would get under my skin and that is all she gave me. You damn right that was enough to get my skin boiling because of course my mind took it to the place where the worst lives and I continued to press her while she showered.

Water is covering my floor because I have the gotdamn shower door wide open because I want to see where she is washing the most. "So this is a fucking game to you I see, I asked you a question, did you go and see Alexander?!" She continues to wash and shake her head at the same time with a disgusted look on her face and that just pissed me off even more. I don't know why the thought of her being with someone else has gotten me riled up like it has.

My guilty conscience is definitely getting the best of me and it really isn't any fun when the rabbit has the gun but I want to know if my pussy has been touched tonight so I take off my clothes and I get in the motherfucking shower with her and begin to kiss her because I want to see how she will react. She does her best to avoid my lips but she's not saying No and giving me tongue. I reach around her waist and place my hand on her pussy and begin to rub on her soapy clit while the other is on her breast and she's getting in to it but still trying to give me attitude.

"You think you are going to get this pussy don't you? You don't deserve this." And she grabs my now swollen wet dick and squeezes it hard. I let out a gasp and although it hurt it also gave my thickness a rush. The water is streaming down our wet bodies and we are fighting for position in the shower.

Every time I try to grab her wet soapy behind she manages to slip away while still raising her ass up for me to get it. We are completely mad with each other; there is still a sense of fire between us that this water cannot put out. "You better not had gone to see Alexander Olivia, don't you fucking do that to me," While fingering her hot hole.

She cocks her leg up on the wall so that I could use more than one finger inside her. "Ahhhhhhh, Kayne, yes baby, stick it up in there baby!" She turns after a few seconds of me manipulating her G-Spot and says, "I'm going to show you why you shouldn't be lying to me Kayne," and she bends down in the shower and places my full erect dick in her mouth and begins to suck me like my head had sugar on the tip. I didn't know what was saliva and what was water but my dick and balls was slippery and shiny and she took every inch of me down her warm throat. It's getting real sensitive now and I'm trying to place my hands on the shower walls so I won't fall.

Water has flooded the bathroom floor but we don't care as we are about to fuck in our own swimming pool. "Wherever you were she will never suck your dick like this! And she begins to suck me fast while jacking me off. I can't take this shit. I pick her up and we get of the shower and lay right on the floor. She already knows where my mind is and opens her legs wide so that her pink spreads like a blooming flower.

Dick rock hard and ready to dive in, I slide inside her and she let out a moan that could heard throughout the house. "Give me this dick, fuck me good and cum in me baby." She knows I love to hear her say that as it gets my dick even harder and normally I would go and put on a condom but this time I wanted to feel her warmth and she had told me days before she wasn't ovulating.

I place my hands underneath her juicy wet ass and pull her close to me so that every inch I had she would feel in her stomach.. The sensitivity was getting closer and we both know what that meant as she could see the excitement in my eyes. I'm now biting my bottom lip as we are in a rhythmic wet body slapping match. Water is everywhere and we are sliding all over the floor. Her pussy has creamed and is now flowing in the pool of water we are splashing in. This electricity can't be matched and this woman turns me on.

After an hour of animalistic fucking on the floor we got back in the shower and washed off our angry sex. There wasn't any more talk of the night before and I'm not sure if it will come up again. All I know is this woman loves me and she makes me feel a certain kind of way. The thought of her giving away this loving will drive me absolutely crazy and from her response, she feels the same way. There were no more games played as we slept the whole day away in each other's arms.

CHAPTER 5
WATCH YOUR BACK

After an extended nap, I decided to get up and check my emails and look over my finances. I kiss Olivia on the forehead while she remained asleep and I went into the living room closing the bedroom door behind me.

Olivia is showing me something different about her daily, some of it I love, some of it I'm wary of. The point remains, she loves me like no other and she doesn't want to share my time with anyone or anything and that is going be a problem as I see the red flags waving in the wind. I log into my computer under my private Cocksman files and notice that I had hundreds of unread mail.

I sift thru the subject lines as they all are inquiring about my services and when they could make an appointment but there was no way in hell that I was going to oblige even half of them but there was one subject line that caught my eye which read, " *Wild Card Applying*".

Now, I'm not usually moved by the unknown but there was something about his subject line that made me want to open the email and read it.

"Hello Kayne, I hope that you get this email soon because I was told that your services were available and worth the money. I have never reached out to a service like this before because I'm very private but my husband does not do it for me sexually anymore and although I'm not the cheating type I'm interested in finding out why you have such a mystique about you in bed. I'm fighting myself as I'm writing this because I know that it's wrong but on the other hand my pussy is soaking wet and throbbing thinking about the things I've heard that you do to women and I'm curious. I'm sure that your schedule is very busy and you may or may not take me up my offer but I will pay you just to meet with you first as money is no problem for me. My husband is very wealthy. And if you don't believe this to be a serious inquiry, you respond with how much it will take to meet with you and what account I should transfer the money to. Within an hours' time, your account should reflect what is required for us to meet………Sincerely, The Wild Card…"

I have had many requests for my services but I must say that this was different and quite interesting. This woman is going to pay me whatever amount I sent back to her without any problem just to meet with me? This has to be a joke and I want to call her bluff but something doesn't sit quite right with me. Why did she sign, "*The*

Wild Card?" What is that supposed to mean? *Is this even a real woman?* Is this a joke?

Nonetheless, I place this email in a private saved folder so that I could come back to it later and I continue to go thru the rest of my mail to see with whom I could get back on the clock with.

Olivia has gotten up now as I hear the bedroom door open and I quickly close my Cocksman Files and go to my banking information before she makes it over to the couch. "What are you doing baby?" she ask, while still yawning. "Just checking my bank account love and from the looks of it, I'm getting low, wait what is this?" I see that there was a withdrawal for six hundred dollars from my account and I know that I didn't do it. "This can't be right, why in the hell am I missing $600?" As I scroll down looking at my history, I'm hoping to find a bill that was automatically withdrawn and I just forgot about it and that be the reason why my money is gone but I see nothing.

I pick up the phone to call my bank and before I could finish dialing the number Olivia speaks. "Kayne, I withdrew that money." Now I'm confused because I'm trying to figure out when she did it, how she knew my pin number and what did she need that much money for?

Before I respond and go off the handle, I go and look at the date the withdrawal was posted and see that it was last night!

"How did you get my card Olivia? How do you even know my pin number? What did you need with six hundred dollars last night?" She sees that I'm heated and about to blow a fuse so she tries to console me first by putting her hand on my thigh, I move her hand immediately because consoling wasn't going to do the job. I wanted some fucking answers.

"You left your wallet on the counter and I came across your pin from some paperwork that was around the house when I was cleaning. She answered two of my questions but clearly attempted to avoid the third, so I ask her again in a tone that could be heard in Arizona.

"WHAT IN THE HELL DID YOU NEED WITH $600 DOLLARS?" as I look at the time of the withdrawal on my computer, "3:30 IN THE MOTHERFUCKING MORNING OLIVIA?!!!!" She just looks at me and doesn't answer.

I am mad as hell because I can't believe she stole my wallet. Yes, she stole it and withdrew my money from my account. Yes, my damn account! I love her true indeed but I will not be dealing with this type of sneaky shit and she will know that after tonight. She's looking at me with her soft eyes and is visibly shaken because I had never shown her this side of me before.

She knows she has fucked up but I'm not caring about the doe eyed shit; I want to know where my money went and when I'm going to get it back.

"I owed someone some money and if I didn't get it back to them something was going to happen to me and I knew you had it. I promise I'll get it back to you as soon as I can."

My first mind wants to ask her, "How in the hell do you know I had it and my second question is, Who do you owe money too and why my money was used to pay your debt and on top of that, what was going to happen to her if it wasn't paid back?" I was eager to hear more of her response so I sit and wait with baited breath.

"You are not going to want to hear this Kayne but I owed Alexander some money and he text me the other day saying that if I didn't return it by last night he was going to come and find me." I'm looking at her with a shocked look on my face.

"So you took money from my account without asking or even telling me to pay a debt back to a man you use to fuck?" "Why is he still calling you anyways, you never mentioned this to me?"

Now all kinds of thoughts are going thru my head because obviously she has been keeping secrets of her own but how can I blame her as I'm doing the same exact thing but hers is in the forefront now, we are not talking about my slick shit.

"He won't stop calling or texting me. Everyday it's a threat and I haven't told you because I didn't know how you would react. I just don't want anyone to get hurt, especially you so I didn't want to tell you Kayne, please understand." I can't and will never understand. I don't need her protecting me nor do I want her having ANY dealings with Alexander and I know what I have to do to rectify this situation.

"Call this motherfucker now and give me the phone Olivia!" She is showing hesitation so I walk into the bedroom and grab her phone to do it myself. As I'm scrolling thru her phone I'm seeing all kinds of names with stars beside them which strikes me as odd but I was too mad to even question her about it right then. My main focus is finding his number in her cell so that I could call him. "I don't see his number. Where is it? What do you have it under?" She remains reluctant while trying to grab her phone away from me but I wasn't having it.

"It's not in there, I erased it!" Pissed off now because she is clearly playing games with me I say to her, "Call him right now, you know the damn number or I'm going over there to find out what the hell is going on!"

Obviously that got her attention because she asks for her phone and begins to dial the number. I could hear the phone ring so I grab it from her because I wanted him to hear my voice as soon as he answered. It's now at three rings and still no answer. "Kayne just hang up, I promise I will handle this."

Ignoring what she is saying, it's now on the fourth ring and then I hear a voice but it's his voicemail picking up. I decided not to leave a message because I didn't want to give his ass a heads up and I knew if he saw a missed called from Olivia he would call back. I'm furious as hell as I walk to the bedroom to put on some clothes to leave, she asks me, "Where are you going?"

Worried that I may be headed to Alexander's, she tries to stand in my way and keep me from leaving. "Don't do this. Don't go over there. Please let me handle this Kayne. Trust me; you don't know what he is capable of!"

It's quite obvious she doesn't know what I'm capable of either because if she did, she wouldn't be giving me this advice.

"And I'm taking your phone with me just in case he calls!" She's fighting to get her phone from me but I'm keeping it away from her. She sees that this is a no win situation and stops the fight; I leave the house slamming the door in her face. I can't believe she has been keeping information from me and what does he have on her that she had to pay him money?

This relationship is turning out to be something awkwardly entertaining and although I've gotten plenty signs to run away from this travesty in the making, I stay around like a fool, refusing to listen, because my heart is softer than my hard head and maybe I'm just a sucker for what I think is true love.

As I'm driving to nowhere, my phone rings. I look at the screen and it's Jasmine. I pick up, "Jasmine, how are you today?" She gets right into it. "Kayne today is my last day of work and I will be checking out. What time will you be able to come and pick me up? I will be done in a couple of hours and I'm looking forward to spending the next couple of days with you before I return home." Her coming to stay at my home is definitely not a possibility so let me dig into my bag of lies and see what I can pull out? "Well as of last night, I had some pipes burst in my kitchen that caused water damage so I'm out of my own home now and going to a hotel for the next couple of days until the repairs are finished." She hesitates a bit before she responds, "Oh, Ok, well I can book a few more nights here and you can come and stay with me." Being the gentleman that I am as well as the lying soul, I decided to take on the financial burden to pay for the room myself, "I'll take care of it Jasmine, you need not to worry, and I'll come by the hotel in a couple of hours."

There you have it, I just put myself in an awkward situation that will have to be explained to Olivia but who gives a damn at this point. She stole my card and used my money to pay back Alexander, that's enough for me to be mad enough not to want to come home for a couple of days and just like that I have created the thesis for Jasmine and I to write this Chronicle that has been on my mind since Mobay.

As I hang up the phone with her and deciding that I better go and pick up some clothes and toiletries for my two day getaway, Olivia's phones rings, I pick it up and see that it's the number that we called. It's Alexander and he is about to be in for a very big surprise. I answer the call but remain silent at first. "I see I missed your call baby, you missing what I gave you the other night?" What in the hell does he mean by that shit?!!!! I couldn't hold my silence any longer.

"You just don't get it do you motherfucker? You remain insistent on being second best to me. I'm everywhere and this will be your last time calling this number. And what do you mean is she missing what you gave her last night?"

You could hear him breathing on the other end of the line because my voice was not the one he was expecting.

"Kayne, you bitch ass motherfucker. So now you are stealing her phone? You're trying to keep her from talking to me again? Guess what, you can keep on trying my man because I got something on her. She has to talk to me and deal with me and trust me Kayne, you don't want to know what I am referring to. Just know she enjoyed it and we will do it again and by the way….THANK YOU for the money, she told me she got it out of your account!"

I guess me whooping his ass didn't leave an imprint like I thought it did because the reckless shit that is coming out of his mouth right now is leading me to believe that her dealings with him are more than what she is telling me.

"Did you fuck her?!!! Did you fuck her motherfucker?!!!!" Alexander could be heard laughing on the other end because he can hear my concern and he played into it.

"Listen Kayne, if you are everywhere, so am I. Look over on your right." And as plain as day, this bitch ass "Stanley" is driving right next to me as he nods his head and makes a sign of a gun with his hands while winking his eye.

"Watch your back Kayne…..I SEEEEEEE YOU!!!!!" and hangs up the phone while exiting the freeway on the opposite side and leaving me in the now congested freeways of Los Angeles. This was no damn coincidence. Has Alexander been following me? Does he know where we live? Olivia told me that I had no idea how far he would go to get and keep her but for the first today, I believed that he may be just as crazy as the picture he is painting. I will take his words into consideration and definitely watch my fucking back.

CHAPTER 6

JASMINE CHRONICLE

What better way to try and get this freeway episode off of my mind than to be getting ready to spend two days with Jasmine. I think I've caused enough strife to keep Olivia off of my back where me being away will be warranted.

As I'm pulling up at the hotel, I can feel my muscle hardening. He must know he's back in a familiar place where he should have been let free and he smells her pheromones from a distance.

I sit for a moment so that he can gain his normalcy and go back into hiding because I surely wouldn't want to walk in announcing my intentions. My phone begins to ring and as I look at the screen to see who it is and I notice it's my home number so I pick up and answer, "Yes Olivia, what do you want?" "Kayne, where are you? Did you go over to Alexander's? What did he say to you?" Now why in the hell is she so worried about those things especially if he had told me something?

"Why does it matter? I'm sure you will find a way to contact him and ask him yourself, that is what your sneaky ass has been doing all along anyways." Yes, I'm pouring it on for the buildup and every time she responds I'm giving her more. "Kayne, did you go? You're not answering me, please tell me that you didn't and you are just taking a ride to cool off."

Part of me is really pissed because it is obvious there's something that I need to know but she is not telling me. The only way I'm going to get the information is if I ask Alexander himself but I'm going to do a little fishing anyway just to see if she will bite.

"It doesn't matter Olivia, just know this, I know and the shit isn't cool. You could have told me." There is a long sigh in between her breaths. Whatever she thought I knew she's acting like she's about to confess something to me. "I'm sorry Kayne, I'll be out of the house before you get home, I wanted to tell you myself but now you know." What the hell!!!! Yes, I want her to elaborate but not tonight, I still need to use this moment to be out of the house and as much as my curiosity is biting my ass right now I'm going to stay on track.

"No need for you to leave, I'm going to stay away myself. I need some time to ingest all of this. There will be no need for you to even contact me; I'll call you when I'm ready to talk." Of course she wasn't having that even though she thought I knew about the rouse she had been hiding. 'What do you mean don't try and contact you? Where in the hell are you going to be? Let me know Kayne, don't play these fucking games with me."

I'm not budging on this so I continue to put fire behind it. At the same time, I get a text from Jasmine asking me was I close. I reply, *Yes I'm in the parking lot now and I'm coming up* before I respond back to Olivia.

"Listen, you want to keep secrets from me then consider this the payback. I said I'll call you when I'm ready to talk and if you try and call you will receive my voicemail. I'm hanging up now!"

And while I'm pressing end I could hear her calling my name. Now the tone is set. I'm free and clear for the next two days without having to worry about appeasing Olivia or running off prematurely. What I've been dreaming about is definitely going to happen and I can't wait. I reach in the backseat and grab my bag for my stay and I head to the room. I'm having the same feeling like I had as a teenager. These butterflies are doing flips in my stomach and I'm wondering why? I've been with hundreds of women and I've always been at ease so I don't know what the difference is tonight.

The closer I get, the crazier those wings are flapping and now I'm at the door and guess who has awaken again? Yep, it's him and he is ready. Before I knock on this door I reach down my Nike runner sweats and shift him so that he will lie down because I don't want her to see me like that when she opens the door.

Jasmine has a class about her and I'm not going to play her like that. I knock on the door and wait for her to answer. After a few seconds, I knock again and the door opens but she's nowhere in sight. The room is dimly lit and *Adore* by Prince is playing in the background. How in the hell did she know that Prince is my mood starter and my favorite artist? I walk in and the door is closed behind me. I turn around and oh my God!!!!! This woman is totally naked. She has her hair in a ponytail which is another favorite of mine.

I can remember as a young boy I would ask my mother to wear her hair in a ponytail because I thought she looked so pretty and here is Jasmine in all of her nakedness making me feel right at home. No words are exchanged at first. She grabs my bag and walks it over to the closet and puts it down. I'm marveling at the shape of this woman's body. All of her curves are meeting symmetrically like waves from the ocean with very little ruffles. Yes, she has class alright!!!The kind of class that is about to get her some of the best dick this side of the Mississippi.

"Jasmine I wasn't expecting this baby, "as she walks over to the bed and pulls down the comforter and sheets. Seductively she says to me, "Kayne take off your clothes and go and shower, I left it running for you." She didn't have to ask me twice to disrobe and that's exactly what I did.

I began to take off everything while she just stood there and watched me. She sat at the foot of the bed with her legs spread wide open and watched. When I got to my sweats and dropped them to the floor she bit her bottom lip and I noticed that she had now placed her finger on her clit and was rubbing it in a circular motion. My dick had risen to all of his inches way past my navel and he was ready to go.

"Hurry back Kayne, I don't want to waste any more minutes on this. You have been on my mind since Jamaica. I've got to feel that!" and she lay back on the bed with her finger inside of her. I hurry to the shower to get fresh and clean because envisioning her full lips on the head of my swollen dick is becoming more than I can handle. My excitement will not get the best me and I don't want to get inside of her and drop a fast load. So, I grabbed some of the gel soap and put it all over my tool and I jacked off. I closed my eyes and imagined my dream about her in Jamaica and before I knew it I had let out the biggest load of premium cum and watched it flow down the drain of the shower.

I finished showering and dried off. My rock was still hard but not as hard as it was before I got in. I had no worries though because I knew she would stimulate me and get me back exactly where I needed to be. I can't believe this is about to go down right now. I guess my preconceived thoughts that I had about her were either wrong or premature. She's a woman just like any other and she wants dick too.

Jasmine is still classy but she threw that shit out of the window when she opened that door naked. There she is lying on the bed as her fingers are shining from all of her wetness. She started without me and had made a gigantic wet spot in the bed but that's ok; I like playing catch-up. I go and lay beside her and begin to softly kiss her neck and take the other hand to rub on her full size D's.

Her breathing is getting heavy as she is grinding the air. My dick is trying to make its way to split her ass in two but I position myself so that I can keep him at ease. I go to part her legs and she looks at me and says, "You be still, I want control over you." As she reaches under her pillow and grabs a long black satin scarf. I had never been in this situation before because I am always in control but tonight it's going to be different.

She asked me, "Can I have my way with you Kayne?" And as much as I fought the thought of it I decided that tonight I was going to relinquish my control to her. She straddles me on the bed while grabbing a bottle of oil and poured it all over my body slowly rubbing it on me while whispering to me, "You are so damn sexy Kayne."

Her tongue is warm and she knows how to use it. Fuck this woman is making me feel a certain kind of way and my dick is hard as shit. I so want to take her now and put all of me inside of her but I can't. She wanted control and I'm going to lay here and see what the hell she's going to do with it.

She now has her hand on the shaft of my swollen manhood. She takes the bottle of oil and drops a few ounces over him and makes it look like raindrops falling on my head. She takes her oily thumb and is slowly rubs me causing me to squirm. This shit feels so damn good and she knows I'm enjoying it. Every muscle in me wants to grab her and just feed her my dick by the pound but she's doing a great job controlling this situation. She's maneuvering without saying a word as her eyes are doing all the talking. Now she's using her tongue as a paintbrush to paint the canvas of my oily body.

I go to grab her head to lead her where I want but she's not having that. She nods her head NO and goes back to painting. She grabs my right thigh and says, "Lift your legs for me."

I follow her directions and do just that. She begins to lick my inner thigh while sucking on it. This is driving me bat crazy and my dick doesn't know if he's coming or going and again I make an attempt to grab her and she gives me a look of, *What did I say the first damn time?*

I guess by this point she's not going to trust my discipline and she grabs that long black scarf and reaches for both of my hands and tie them together. She wasn't shy about it either, she didn't want me to touch her while she was working and that damn knot was tight. She gives me another look and says, "Relax, the night is just beginning." I don't know who this Jasmine is because it definitely wasn't the Jasmine I met on the island but I'm selfish and I want them both.

Jasmine made it to my nipples; she's sucking on them like a man would suck on a woman's. I never really thought about how that would make me feel but I think she's about to make me cum doing it.."AHHHHHHHHHH, fuck Jasmine, No baby, No!" but she doesn't listen and she keeps applying wet, oily saliva filled pressure to my nipples while swirling her tongue on them.

She was pulling a *Kanye move on me* in this damn bed and I'm allowing this shit to go down? She knows what is about to happen so she sits up and watches. I look down at my throbbing head and its erupting small bursts of excitement. She quickly grabs my balls with force and stops the flow. "Not all of it just yet Kayne. Save some."

At this point I'm gone. Never have I ejaculated from a woman sucking on my nipples. Maybe it was the buildup of what she has been doing. Hell, I shouldn't have cum like this in the first place, that's why I rubbed one out in the shower. She is damn good and I'm looking at her like, *Who in the hell are you?*

She sits on my stomach and bends over to kiss me. Her mouth is warm and wet; her tongue knew how to move but I can't grab or caress her ass because I'm tied up. She whispers in my ear, "Spread your legs wide now." And like a good listener, I do so. My dick is pointing straight at the ceiling despite its left curve and she just stared at it like it was a work of art. It looks like she's trying to make up her mind what she wants to do with it.

I lay back and close my eyes as whatever decision she was about to make I was going to be all for it. She decides to put it in her mouth. Damn, it's warm, it's wet and it feels like a pussy. I want to grab her head so fucking bad but my gotdamn hands are still tied.

She begins to suck me with a rhythm like I had never had before. There were no hands involved either; every time she got to the base of my dick a pool of saliva would gather around my balls.

" Baby stop, please stop…Oh shit please slow down!" but she didn't listen and in a few more slurps of my manhood, I exploded again but she didn't stop, she just let in run out of the sides of her mouth like a champion. Jasmine was nasty with it and I loved it.

Men are visual creatures and the nastier the scene, the better the view and from my vantage point, oh what a view it was. "This shit has never happened before Jasmine, what are you doing to me?" With a serious look on her face she replied, "I'm bringing you back home the island way" and proceeded to suck me.

I can't take this anymore. She has made me cum twice in a matter of minutes. I want to turn her ass over and give her the business but I can't get my gotdamn hands free from this marine knot she has assembled.

I look at my dick and he's looking back at me as if to say, " *What the fuck is going on here Kayne? This is not like us!!!"*

I surrendered to her wishes a while ago so now I'm just along for the ride. She grabs the base of my balls again and stops my flow. She had this down to a science. She stretches over across the bed and reaches into the drawer. She pulls out a condom. She tears the packet open and places it in her mouth. She gazes at my dick to determine which angle she wants to take to cover my manhood with protection.

She comes back to my mouth and thrusts her tongue deep into my throat and kisses me passionately. Her body is searing and I can smell her pussy boiling in the air; its taking every bit of strength in me not to grab her waist and push every inch inside of her until she surrenders to me but I promised I would let her have her way.

She says to me, "Close your eyes Kayne, "And I do. The room goes quiet and now she blindfolds me. I have never felt vulnerable like this before but I'm loving this show she is putting on for me. She grabs my tied hands and puts her pussy close to where I can place my fingers inside of her.

She inserts two fingers inside of her with ease and it feels like I'm playing in a pool of warm water. She lets out a sigh, "Ahhhhh that feels good Kayne" but I want to be inside of her. She reverses her position in a cowgirl stance. Grabs my rock hard jack hammer and guides my head inside her orifice. It wasn't even three bounces before her body became weak and limp and she squirted all over me.

She had built her arousal threshold up too and came like a hydrant when I pierced her labia. "Are you ready to take over now Kayne?" All I could do was nod my head yes and offer her my hands. She untied the knot and freed me from my captivity; the look in her eyes revealed that the game was about to fucking change.

"You're free now baby; do what you want to do to me Kayne." Why did she say that? I whispered in her ear, 'I want this pussy now", and for the rest of the night we came a total of ten times. Every item on the bed was on the floor. We went thru just about all of the condoms and we both lost about five pounds from all of the pounding and sweating. By the time the sun said hello we decided we wanted to pretend the moon was waving and fell asleep, her body on top of mine with my hands strategically placed on her ass that is overflowing to her hips. It was all that I thought it would be and although the dream seemed real her reality was even better.

CHAPTER 7
THE HEART LOVES WHO IT WANTS

Fireworks in April is what I'll call the night that we just had; the after affects can be seen throughout the hotel room because there wasn't an inch that we didn't cover as Jasmine lay naked on top of the duvet still asleep.

I can only shake my head at what I discovered. After last night I knew that she is definitely a contender and when she plays she plays hard. I must have watched her torso rise and fall for close to an hour before I decided to wake her. Her legs were open and inviting me to taste the night before and I had no problem with that. I slowly pushed them farther apart because I wanted to see all of the honey I was about to eat.

I gently slide my tongue across her clit to see if she would move. The warmth from my heated mouth must have made her pearl tingle a bit because she let out a slight moan but kept her eyes closed. Wanting to get more of a reaction, I plunged my entire tongue deep inside her wet and tangy insides and that did the trick because her eyes popped wide open.

"Good morning baby, I see you're enjoying your morning breakfast." With a mouth full of pussy, I managed to respond, "Oh yes I am. Now you just lay back and close your eyes." She sits up a little and asks, "Shouldn't I go and clean up first so that you can have me fresh?" "Mandingos don't worry about such things when they are in warrior mode, I said to her, There won't be any need for that Jasmine, I'll clean you up myself," and I went back to devouring her pussy as if it would be my last meal.

She tasted even better after the night we had and I'm guessing it's because those sweet Jamaican juices had stewed overnight and made a tasty roux so I made myself right at home. She scratched and crawled all over the bed trying to get away from my feasting but I wouldn't let her escape.

"Yuh gwan be still pon deh dey bed and mey gwan eat yah like dere is nuh more!" She understood exactly what I meant by that and relaxed even more. She put her hands under her knees and pulls them toward her chest and left me with all pussy and ass to behold. I could tell she was about to pitch me her best and I was ready to catch her fast ball.

After giving her simultaneous lickings from her pussy to her ass I could see her stomach tightening as she was preparing to let go. I sucked harder and deeper while fingering her at the same time. This drove her crazy.

"Kayne, you are about to get splashed, you better stop, you better pull away baby…oh shit, you better stop Kayne!!!!." I can be a hard head when I want to be and I was going to show her just how much of a hard head I could be. I started flickering my tongue on her swollen pearl and that took her West Indian ass over the edge and she let me have it.

While my entire mouth was over her wet dripping sweet spot, she squirted at least eight ounces of her sugary excitement all over my mouth and face. I had a look of an intense ferocious lion protecting his lioness and wiped my mouth of some of the juices I didn't swallow. "I want that every time, Jasmine, don't you hold back and cheat me. You give me all of that nectar, do you hear me?" She's convulsing and her body is still shaking from the orgasms and nods yes to my request. 'Now you go and clean yourself up." She sits up in the bed and pulls me close to her.

"Kayne, you were absolutely amazing and exactly what I thought you were going to be. I've masturbated at the thought of feeling you since we've met and now I know this is a feeling that I could get used to." Then she gets up and heads to the bathroom to shower. I lay in bed in her wet spot as the aroma of fresh ejaculation fills the room and I wonder how it would be to be with her exclusively. There's a familiarity with her that I don't have with Olivia. We share a common bond and I have to admit that after having sex with her, Olivia has nothing on this woman. I'm just attracted to everything about Jasmine.

Of course I still have to learn more about her because she could have a past like Olivia but something tells me, she doesn't. She may be a better fit for me. Why couldn't I have met her before Olivia? There's always a monkey wrench being thrown into what could have been perfection but I guess my life wasn't meant to be easy. The hard road is what I'm use to and that exactly how it's going to remain. Jasmine has finished showering and comes back into the room and sits on the bed. "Wow, what a way to be awaken, you are very good with that tongue." And she kisses me. "So what do you want to do today? It's supposed to be gorgeous weather, let's get out and see the city."

Careful in how I respond because there are parts of the city I'm going to stay away from because of proximity so I'll suggest someplace far out. "Let's drive up the coast to Malibu and have lunch overlooking the ocean." She must have liked the idea because her face lit up and a smile took over, "Perfect baby, go clean up and let's start our day." And she goes to get dressed. As she remains preoccupied getting dainty for our outing, I get my phone and turn it on to see if I had any messages or emails. As soon as it powers up, I noticed I had 10 voicemails and a few unread emails. The messages were from Olivia. I guess she didn't believe that I would not be coming home or answering her calls.

    I want to hear the messages and what she had to say but it will have to wait. The emails on the other hand, I needed to address immediately. One was spam, another was from my bank and the other was from the "Wild Card".

    I look to see what Jasmine was doing; she had made her way into the bathroom doing her hair. I had a few minutes to investigate what was in the email. *"Kayne, I haven't heard from you yet and I was hoping that I would have already. Maybe you don't think I'm serious about my inquiry so this is what I'm going to do. You double that number of what it would have taken to have met with me and give me your routing and account number and Ill deposit it immediately. I'm at my bank right now and I won't leave the parking lot until I get a response from you.*

"

I can't believe this. Is this woman serious? I go and look at the email from my bank and see the monthly statement attached and I was a bit low on funds. I hadn't been on the clock in a while and my savings were depleting fast. I needed cash like yesterday so I may have to see about this wild card. I glance up and notice that Jasmine is still doing her hair when, she calls out, "Baby, we are losing sun, let's get ready!" I respond back, "Just returning some important emails," I'm getting in the shower right after." I go back to the email and respond. "*We will see if you are serious Wild Card. Here is my bank routing and account number. The cost will be 5K just to meet*" and I press send. I put my phone away and head to the shower to get ready.

It's a little past noon now and we are headed toward Malibu. It's a beautiful day in LA; the weather is perfect. Music is blasting and Jasmine has her Prada Oversized Cat Eye sunglasses on, her hand is rubbing my thigh and we're both just taking in the moment.

We are 50 miles away from our destination which gave us ample time to engage in conversations that was overlooked last night due to our other interests. "So how have you been Kayne, what's been going on and why are you single again?" The truth could set me free but my selfishness will keep my ass captive for now and I say to her, "Relationships complicate my life these days so I stay as far away from them as possible for fear that I may become lost in the Love that truly doesn't exist." She removes her hand from my thigh while she takes in what I've just said.

"I remember you being very poetic with words Kayne and that's what I always thought about when you came to mind. It's a shame that the pain that you are clearly feeling cannot be washed away like sand into the ocean. New tides brings different patterns, do you know that?" I knew what she meant and she was showing me that she could be a wordsmith too when it came to the heart. "You are absolutely right Jasmine and I agree with you, I guess it will have to be a very special woman to get me back to a place where my heart is comfortable to breathe again but until then, it will keep skipping beats on its own because it's afraid to rely on itself.

It's been suffocated so much that normal breathing patterns don't exist anymore." She laid her head back on my leather seats and glance out of the window as I drive. Prince's, *The Beautiful Ones* is playing in the background, the conversation has toned down and I see that her mind is in silent rotation. We have about 30 miles to go and she looks over to me, "Kayne I can be the one, I just need for you to be open to that possibility? I'm not her. I won't hurt you and I need you to know that because it's obvious after last night she's not the one you want to be with." She got me. She sees right thru me and I know she's smarter than she's letting on, thinking I'm keeping her from something and she's slick with it too. She has a feeling I have something going on but still fucks me good anyway.

Jasmine was strategic with her moves and she had me. I'm going to tell her about Olivia right now. She has pretty much given me the green light to do so. This is my chance to come clean so here goes but just as I was about to speak my truth her cell phone rings and it's her job.

Timing is always against me when it comes to the reveal but I didn't force it. She talked for the rest of the ride until we pulled up to the seaside restaurant in Malibu.

While sitting in front of the pacific bay window overlooking the ocean we are sharing moments with laughter, good food and her drinks. At this moment, life is wonderful; I have forgotten about my life back in Los Angeles. I had the same feeling when I was in Jamaica when we met and I liked it. Jasmine had a sense of humor too which was a total turn on for me. We discussed her family life in more detail and I found out that her family not only came from money back home in Jamaica as Sugar Kane proprietors but her father and uncles were also government officials. She also has an advanced educational background; Jasmine was a very intelligent woman who held two degrees from Princeton and Dartmouth. She was more refined than Olivia and captivating as I hung onto every word she spoke.

This is what I needed to replenish my soul and this is the woman my mother should be meeting .This was the woman who should have been working at the hotel and not that sneaky ass Olivia who steals my fucking money to pay a debt to an old lover!

Jasmine is right, she is not Olivia, far from it but the heart loves who it wants when it wants but I can foresee a tug of war in the very near future if I continue to deal with Jasmine. She is making it hard for me to close my eyes to the opportunity that is clearly presenting itself to me. "Jasmine, I want you to know something. There hasn't been a day since we've met that I haven't thought about you. There's something about you that draws me in and I'm refusing to fight it because I know you are good for me.

I don't know how you feel about what I'm saying right now but there's something about you I can't escape and don't want to let go." She just stares at me while holding her glass of wine. She takes a sip and says, "Then don't let me go." For the rest of that day we finished our lunch, held hands, watched the wave's crash the shore and laughed through conversation.

She never did come back to that question and I never brought it up again. She had a feeling there was someone else in my life and that was good enough for me. She was calm to me with no storm in sight; I loved it. It's late in the afternoon now and we have decided to head back to the Hotel for the night. I asked if she wanted to go anyplace else; she declined and said she would rather spend her last night in bed in my arms. "I want you to just make love to me tonight Kayne, will you do that?"

There was no question I could do that and I couldn't wait to get back to the room. While driving along the winding roads back to the city and watching a theater of stars shining bright Jasmine reaches over into my lap and unzips my jeans. "Baby, you see I'm driving, what are you about to do?" She smiles and says, "And you are a good driver too, so keep it up." And before I knew it, she had taken me in her mouth and sucked me all the way down

PCH highway. By the time we hit the city limits she had swallowed what she was trying to get out of me and was proud of it. When she finished, she just bobbed her head to the music that was playing while placing my tool back into my pants. She was a quiet beast who was making a definite point that she was a force to be reckoned with.

Back in the room, all showered and relaxing in bed watching T.V. naked, Jasmine decides to turn the conversation back on. "Kayne, do you always see yourself living here in Los Angeles or could you go back to the island?"

She raised a very good question because if I wasn't a Cocksman, I would love to be in the countryside of Mo Bay but there would be no way in hell I could pull that off on the island. The familiarity alone would get me caught up and that's just not a place where I would want to take this horrible soul killer to. Jamaica is a place to rest, regain your peace, and not put it up for sale. "I would love to go back to the island and live the rest of my days Jasmine but I would have to have my money right in order to do so. I think about leaving here all the time actually. This isn't a place that you would want to live if you want peace. The city never wakes up because it never sleeps and you can get caught up here." Taking in all I had said she says with a serious tone, "I don't know what is going to happen or if anything can happen with you and me but I do know this, you interest me a great deal and I want to learn more. I want to be with you Kayne and if there is ever a day that you do return back to Ja I want to share those moments with you."

Now that is one thing that I love about Jasmine. She doesn't hesitate to let me know how she feels and her intentions. You have to respect her nobility when it comes to that; I appreciated that about her.

She has not asked me about my job nor elaborated on my current love fiasco and quite frankly, I truly hope she doesn't. Maybe all of this will work out in my favor and we'll find a way to be together. Maybe Jasmine is just like Olivia and turns me the hell off so I can be done with the both of them. Maybe I need to just be alone and be happy with the fact that I'm no good for anyone because my chances at getting it right faded away when I learned that being a Cocksman was way more exciting than being normal.

I'm nowhere near normal and she has no clue the depth of complication I could present in her life. I could only respond by saying to her, "Time is on our side baby and we will see where the navigation will take us." And I kiss her softly on her lips. She places her hands behind my head, pulls me close to her body and returns the same sentiments. "I leave tomorrow Kayne but I will be back. I need more from you, I want more from you and I want us to explore those possibilities. I'm not seeing anyone so I will ask this of you. If you are available, I want you for me, if you are not available then fix that problem and come home." I knew what she meant when she said come home. Home is my roots. Home is Jasmine. Home is the bloodline we share.

We made slow passionate love for the remainder of the night like we didn't want to share the world with anyone else. When morning arrived, Jasmine was already up, dressed and ready to meet the car service to head out. She kisses me on the forehead to wake me. "Baby, I have to go now, I asked for a late checkout so you can sleep in.

I really enjoyed my time with you and I look forward to more moments like the ones we have shared. I want to experience what it will be like to love you Kayne…..All of you. I will call you when I land."

And just like that she grabs her bags and heads toward the door. Before she opens it to leave I give her my word, "The next time we see each other Jasmine it will be the start of forever, I promise you." She gives me that smile again that melts everything around me and walks out the door. She leaves me lying in bed wondering what in the fuck did I just say? I lay in bed for a few more hours then I reach for my phone to turn it on. I see that I have several messages with the majority being from my home phone. I'm sure this won't be nice when I get home and I'm not so sure that I'm ready to return just yet. I'll just let her sweat her fucking mistake out a little longer.

I could get me a room for another night just to pour it on thick or I could go back and deal with the drama that awaits me. An email alert buzzes my phone and I open it. It's one from my Cocksman email account and the other from my bank. I open the bank email first and I'll be damned. The money is there like *The Wild Card* said it would be and it showed it was deposited yesterday after I sent her the email.

DAMN!! She paid the money I asked for. This is serious now and since I'm a man of my word, it's time to meet. I opened her email and it read, *"Hello Kayne, the money was deposited like I said it would be. Now I hope that we can meet soon. I'm free tomorrow; I'll be having lunch in Marina Del Ray at noon at the Beachside Bar Restaurant. I'm expecting to see you there."* This woman has just deposited 10K in my account without a question and all she wants to do is meet for now. As crazy as this sound, I'm going to do it and not renege. Hell, if she has money like that there's no telling what she is willing to spend. I'll rest for a few more minutes, reflect on what Jasmine and I just shared these last couple of days and wonder what the future will hold. One thing is for sure, I'm interested in finding out if she will be a part of it.

CHAPTER 8
THE WILD CARD

I decided to stay out one more night so I got a room at the Marina so that I would be close for my meeting. It was a clear and beautiful day and I was feeling good. I had just spent two fantastic days with Jasmine, had some of the best sex ever and I got paid 10K just to show my face.

Life was good even though I still have to deal with my current situation. I checked my phone again and there were no more messages from Olivia. I guess she got the picture and stopped making an effort to contact me which was fine because I was enjoying myself and really didn't want to discuss that bullshit with her anymore.

The eatery was within walking distance of my hotel so I put on some comfortable attire. I grabbed my Emporio Armani brown tint sunglasses and began my walk toward the restaurant. I knew that I was meeting a woman but I had no other details on what she would be wearing or what she would look like. As I got closer to my destination I noticed that there were a few women standing outside of the entrance looking like they were waiting on someone. Could one of them be this *Wild Card?*

They were pretty attractive and looked like either of them could have been capable of depositing such a large sum of money into my account. I had no clue which one I should make eye contact with so I just walked up and stood firm. I mean, she would reveal herself to me, after all, she knows who I am.

After standing there for about five minutes, nobody saying a word to me, I began to wonder if I had been duped, then a Black Escalade pulls up curbside in front of the restaurant. A driver gets out of the vehicle, comes around and opens the door. "Kayne, thank you for coming, please get in."

From outside of the vehicle all I saw was long brown legs accompanied with Christian Louboutin black Snakilta spiked leather ankle red bottoms on her feet. As I get into the vehicle and got a closer look I realized who my *Wild Card* was. It was the wife of the wealthy Congressman from the party I attended months ago. Regina Landry, the woman who sucked me completely dry in the movie theater. I remembered the card she gave me that clearly stated, *"Until next time";* well I'm guessing the next time is now. This woman was stunning; her mocha brown skin shimmered from the sun rays that crept thru the dark tint. "I told you we would meet again Kayne, can you recall what the name of that movie was?" I could hear the sarcasm float out of her mouth although neither one of us cracked a smile. Now I knew how serious this woman was and it was a pleasure already knowing she and I had connected before. Her story about "not being familiar with this type of behavior" was all a ploy, a lie just to throw me off; however, I knew this could be a very poisonous connection. I was aware that her husband was very powerful and extremely influential and I have to wonder why she would risk losing it all on a sinful tryst with me.

"Up the PCH and please raise the partition", she tells her driver. This lady was a boss and her husband was footing the bill. I'm sure his affluence is financing this meeting but that is her problem to deal with and her comfort level suggests that she has done this before.

As we hit the freeway and the partition is being raised, I see that she is wearing an overcoat that is closed tight at the waist; I'm assuming there's a gift for me underneath.

"So tell me, why did you want to meet me, what is this all about?" She slowly repositions her legs and says very melodically. "Did you think that all I was going to do was suck your dick and that be it Kayne? I want the entire package and your price won't ever be a problem. As a matter of fact, I would like to put you on retainer just for me. I'll pay you for whatever your monthly engagements will cost you plus perks."

I'm sitting here listening to this woman putting in her bid and I must say it's a pretty damn good bid and I'm interested. Hell, she just dropped ten grand in my account just to meet, who's to say she can't do that on a monthly stipend? "So you're saying you want the clock all to yourself and you will pay me graciously for it?" With no hesitation she responds, "That's exactly what I'm saying Kayne. You can still make the same money but it will come from one person who has no limit on the amounts that she can spend. Trust me you may want to seriously think about this proposition."

This does sound good but with good there is always a price to pay. "Tell me Regina, what is the catch? There has to be a catch." She begins to unfasten her belt on that Prada overcoat dress. "There's no catch Kayne. I just want to pay you handsomely for fucking me like I need to be fucked. I'm not getting what I need at home and I have needs. I've heard about you and I want in on a regular basis.

When I call you, we meet. I pay you. You fuck me until I tap out and we both go back home to our separate lives, it's just that simple." I'm still curious, so I ask her, "So what about your husband? How will you pull this off? He is well connected and I'm sure he has his eyes on everything, including the finances. Won't he miss it?"

She opens her coat and reveals a body that is ready to be ravaged. It's obvious she also spends a lot of time in the gym because she is sculpted. "Let me worry about him, I got this under control. Again, it's simple. I'll pay you to make me cum. I don't care about what you have going on in your life. You just get away when you get my call. I'll set everything up. Now is this something that you think you can agree to?"

I'm looking at this woman's body and there's no doubt in my mind I can agree to punishing her pussy and making her feel the way she needs to feel; this could solve my money woes and eliminate me having to sneak out to be on the clock full time with different women.

You damn right I'm going to agree to this transaction. "It's a deal, when do you want to start?" I said that to see if she would bite and it worked. "How much will it take? Give me a number right now." This woman has access to money. I see it and if 10K didn't make her flinch then asking for more shouldn't be a problem but I don't want to price myself out. "Let's just keep it at 10K for now and you also provide the rendezvous locations." She looks at me and opens her legs and says, "Tell you what, if you can make me cum while eating my pussy, I'll make it 15 grand and give you an extra $2500 right now for looking so damn good."

This pussy was juicy and well-manicured. It didn't look like it had many miles on it and it was already crying for me to lick her. So I grabbed both of her legs and spread them as wide as the back seat would allow and I went it. Her juices were sweet and she smelled like French Vanilla. As soon as my tongue hit her clit, her stomach began to flutter like the wings of a Monarch.

"Be still Regina, don't you make a fucking sound. You wanted to see what all the fuss is about and you are paying me a great sum of money. You do what I say now; your ass belongs to me."

She must have loved how I turned the tables on her. So what if she is paying me, she will never own this dick. I will always be in control of it. She is just the highest bidder right to have complete access. "Now hold your legs open and let me see how much of my tongue I can thrust inside of you." She takes my orders and pulls them back toward the window. Pussy and ass are all I see. I can see that it is already pulsating and throbbing in anticipation of me. I continue to plunge my tongue slowly and deeply inside of her while sucking on her swollen clit. "Oh shit Kayne, I can't be quiet baby, I got to talk, I can't keep quiet, suck this pussy baby."

I knew she couldn't keep her mouth closed especially while I'm ravaging her honey. Many women have tried, all have failed. Once I put my tongue to work, you will be at my beckoning call. She starts to rhythmically gyrate her hips to my licking motions and tries to grab the back of my head.

"No……You never touch my head. Matter of fact you put your arms up in the air and you keep them there until I'm finished." She lifts her arms up and I force her legs open wider and I lick her ass. "Oh my gawddddddddddd Kayne!!" She tries to grab my head again. "You are not a good listener are you? You put those fucking hands up like I said, if they come down, I'm going to spank this little ass!"

I begin to fuck her pussy and ass with my tongue with the velocity of a wind storm. Out the window I can see that we are on the Pacific Coast Highway. The coastline is beautiful but not as beautiful as the cream delight that I see oozing from her swollen sweet spot. "You're going to cum very soon baby, trust me, especially when I do this". That's when my tongue game gets serious; I give her the best sucking, pulling and nibbling that she ever had. I placed her clit in my mouth and I sucked it like the sweetest nectar was being released. All of a sudden, I heard her hit the highest note of pleasure while her body begins to shake until her knees hit the floor of the Escalade. "Oh shit….Oh shit……..oh shit……I can't stop cumming!!!! …I can't stop!!!!…It's running down my leg!!!!" Sure enough her juices were dripping down her leg to her red bottom heels.

Her reaction to my masterful cunnilingus has turned me on and I want to cum too. I keep condoms in my pockets for emergencies like this and I pulled one out of my pocket and tore that bitch open. "Oh shit, I didn't expect I was going to get this dick Kayne." As she takes off the coat and unfastens her heels. "I want you to put all of that inside me."

We are now both naked and my dick is hard as a fucking boulder. "How do you want this?" There were no words, she puts her knees in the chair and arches her back. From the back is how she is about to take these inches. I take of my hand and spread her cheeks wide. I prepared her for my entry with one full lick from her clit to her ass and then I made contact with her pussy with force of a Heavyweight's jab. I didn't care to tread softly. I gave her pussy powerful punch which released a deep moan and put her hands on the widows. There was non-stop stroking and moaning as we saturated the leather. Considering we had very limited space, we found ways to make it work.

She turned over on her back and took her beating. "You like this dick don't you? He doesn't fuck you like this does he?" Between catching her breath and caressing her nipples, "Fuck no!!! He doesn't!!! Oh he doesn't!!!! Don't stop Kayne!!!! Fuck me harder!!" And I did that! I gave her a good thrashing and a taste of her own pussy when we tongued kissed each other. She wanted to ride this dick. So I sat back in the seat. She positioned herself backwards on and lowered herself on my tool.

She placed her hands against the partition and braced her feet on the floor and bounced on me like I was a pogo stick. She rode this dick like a bucking cowgirl. She was definitely a *Wild Card* and a screamer too. I know the driver heard us but he kept his professionalism intact and kept driving the sex filled aroma therapy bed on four wheels.

"I'm about to cum again baby, oh god, this dick is amazing!!!!" I'm getting turned on by her enthusiasm and

I started to feel a certain kind of way. She took me there and I felt nasty as fuck so I met her enthusiasm with my own. "When you're about to cum I want you to sit on my face and ride my tongue do you hear me?!" Rapidly, still bouncing on my dick, she responds, "Yes, Baby, Yes!" And I reach around and start to fondle her breast and caress her nipples while kissing down her spine. I knew she was about to explode because I could literally see her scratching the tinted glass partition and sweat was dripping from the nape of her neck.

I was drenched in with sweat; the leather seats were covered in both of our DNA. "Here is comes Kayne!!!!" She jumps up and forces me to lie down. She sits on my face, covering my mouth and rides my stiff tongue and before you know it……..Gulp!!!!! I'm swallowing her release and she is screams, "*SHIT!!!!!!!!!!*" By this time, my cum has made its way to the tip of my shaft and like a gymnast, she positions her body, flips over and rips the condom off of my manhood. She begins to jack and suck me off and swallows all of my protein!

"Fuckkkkkkkkkkkkkkkkkkkkkkkkk!!" I prop myself up and glance down at her cleaning my dick and balls. "Yes, I'll pay for this kind of service anytime Kayne." She wipes her mouth and begins to get dressed. I follow suit and begin to dress too. "Damn woman you are a wild one and I like it." She laughs at my statement while refastening her coat and says, "You have no idea Kayne" and she pulls more money out from the pocket and hands it to me. "You made me cum and gave me dick that I wasn't expecting, so thank you." I take the money not worrying to even count it because I know it's there.

    I have hit the damn jackpot and I love the payout. Let's just hope that I don't crap out and mysteriously no strings pops up after more rendezvous like this takes place.

    By the time we get ourselves together and have small talk I notice that we have returned back to the original spot where I was picked up. The driver gets out and comes to open the door for me. "Thank you Kayne for meeting me for lunch. It was definitely fulfilling; we will do it again." She hands me a cell phone and smiles. "This is for you. There will be no need to use your phone. I'll contact you."

    I grab the phone, place it in my pocket where the money is and I get out. "Until we meet again Regina, have a wonderful evening" and the driver closes the door. Before he walks around to get back in the SUV he looks at me with a smirk on his face and says, "We will be seeing you again Kayne" and he walks away. I'm walking back toward my car thinking about what just transpired and the money I'm about to get from it. Right then, I decided to check my phone. I powered it on and several alerts popped up. I see that I have messages from Olivia and Jasmine. I checked Jasmine's first because she has left me a voicemail. "*Thinking of you Kayne and missing you already, I hope you have given some thought to what we discussed. Come on home, I'll be waiting on you.*"

All I could do was shake my head after listening to her message. I have definitely created more drama than I want to admit and I don't know how I'm going to juggle this. My heart and my work are in shambles but I need them both to co-exist. I don't know how that will work and who will be standing in the end. It's been a few days now and I know I need to get home and face the music with Olivia.

I'm sure it's not going to be pretty but fuck it; my life has never been pretty and ugly is all I know. I text Olivia, *"I'm on my way home, we need to talk"* and press send. Jasmine wants she wants. The *Wild Card* will now be my financier and Olivia will be the thorn in my goddamn side that I don't want to rid myself of. Being me is never easy and being easy can never exist because I will never allow it. Olivia I'm coming home and although I'm coming back with dishonesty attached to the days I've been away, I've still missed you.

CHAPTER 9

OLIVIA HAS HER SUSPICIONS

By the time I get home it is well after midnight and there were no lights on in my home. I get out of the car and proceeded to my door. Before I key in, I place my ear to the door to see if I hear anything. There was no sound so I assumed that Olivia was already in bed.

So I slowly place my key in the door and open it without making the slightest bit of noise. The front room was dark. Thinking I'm in the front room alone, I go over to turn on the light. I flick on the light and low and behold Olivia was standing there; she scared the living shit out me.

"What the hell!!!! Why are you here in the fucking dark and why didn't you say anything when I came in?" You can tell she has been crying because her eyes are swollen and bloodshot red. She has a look on her face that could kill. "So this is how it's going to be Kayne? Where were you and who were you with?" I knew this was going to be a very long night so I head to the back room to get undressed and put on something more comfortable. Olivia is tracking me like a hound and following every step that I make. She continues to rant and ask questions. "I know you see I called your ass. You got my text and why was I going to voicemail Kayne? Who were you with?!!!"

I just look at her without saying a word and I know that my silence is increasing to the temperature in the room but I'm going to let her percolate a bit more before I engage in a war of words. I was a bit hungry, so after putting on some boxers, I walk toward the kitchen and open the fridge to see what I could eat. Like a lap dog, Olivia took pursuit and trailed. Seeing that I'm ignoring her, she hauls off and kicks the refrigerator closed with me still bent over looking in it. "What in the hell is wrong with you?!!!!!!"

So your ass can talk!" Since I'm not going to be eating anything tonight I return to the living room and sit down; she follows. "Listen, Olivia it doesn't matter where I have been. I told you that I wouldn't be answering any of your calls so you shouldn't have expected it. I needed to clear my head and that's what I did, I cleared my head." I guess she must have forgotten that she took my money and gave it to that clown and she has the nerve to have a problem with me not being home.

"I know you are pissed with me Kayne about that money and you have every right to be but I refuse to be treated any kind of way. We are in a relationship dammit and you just don't leave when you get mad." She has a point and I know I shouldn't have done it but how in the hell else would I have gotten out of the house to spend time with Jasmine?

I still have to find out what is going on with her allegiance to Alexander. Before it's all over with that's what I'm going to do but not tonight. I'm exhausted and I really don't care about anything right now so I'll ease the tension and play into her psyche a bit. "You're right Olivia, I'm sorry. I was just angry that you haven't been honest and forthright about your dealings with Alexander and I have to admit, I'm finding it very hard to trust you right now but I love you and I don't like us fighting so let's just get a good night's sleep and discuss this tomorrow, is that ok?"

She is looking at me very funny as if there was something suspicious behind the words I had just spoken and I stared back. Maybe we both were standing out ground but I didn't flinch. I didn't want her to ask me about my two day rendezvous and I know she didn't want me to ask any more about that money. "I'm going to take a shower and go to bed ok?" She grabs my arm before I start to walk away. "You haven't been home Kayne and all you want to do is take a shower? Didn't you miss this?" She starts to remove her clothes but truthfully I was drained and my muscle wasn't budging. It was like he wasn't even interested and that was unlike him.

I don't know what is going on but the Lion in me was lying dormant and I wasn't interested in waking him. She comes closer, puts her arms around me and tries to kiss me but I turn my head to the side.

"What the fuck is wrong with you Kayne? Why are you acting like this? You don't want me anymore? I'm sure I do but truthfully, at this point my interest and thoughts are elsewhere, my manhood has nothing left to offer and I'm completely drained but I can't tell her that. "Olivia, I'm just not in the mood babe. I'm kind of tired and need rest." She was not happy with my response and she puts her clothes back on. "Kayne, you have never turned me down. I don't know what the hell is your problem or what bitch you have been laying up with but I promise you this; if I find out that you are messing over me you will regret it. I promise you that." She turns and walks away leaving me standing there with my head riddled with speculation.

I know she has her suspicions, hell I do too, so I guess we will both be playing detective. Again, I don't know what is going to happen with me, Olivia and the other characters in our steamy saga but I do know this: it's going to be an interesting ride. I guess being the object of rejection was just too much for Olivia because she stormed into the bedroom to gather some clothes as if was about to leave; I stop her in her tracks and ask, "What are you doing?"

"So is this what we are going to do Olivia, go tit for tat?" Still throwing clothing into her bags she looks at me and responds, "Kayne you have never rejected me…. NEVER. I know you and this is not something you would do. I don't know where you were nor who you were with but I damn sure hope it was worth it. I'm not leaving, I'm just going for a ride to clear my head and when I return I will be fine." She continues to pack some of her things.

Now, I'm wondering how in the hell is she going to take a ride because I'm sure not about to let her use my vehicle to go do whatever and see whomever. My curiosity was getting the best of me so I asked, "So who are you leaving with Olivia, who is coming to get you?" As she is placing a pair of her heels in her duffle bag she turns to me and says, "Who says someone is coming to get me?" She cocks her head to the side and continues, "I have my own car now Kayne so I can come and go as I please." Her tone shifts to aggression and pain and she says, "You know you made a lot of sense the other day. You made it perfectly clear to me that without you being a part my life, it wasn't worth shit, that I had nothing to offer. Well those days you were gone, I decided to change that and get my own." She rages on, "Yes, I have my own car now," and saunters toward the door with her Gucci bag on her shoulder, purse on her arm and keys in hand. What…she has a car! How in the hell did she get a car that so quickly? More importantly, who helped her get it was my concern. This woman never ceases to amaze me. There never a dull moment with her. This is the shit I left Jamaica for? Is this what I needed to have in my life? Olivia is starting to cause me more issues than the pleasures.

    Trust is becoming a major issue for me but how in the hell can I be mad when I'm doing the same thing. It's the double standards that we uphold that cause us issues. We are clearly not as in love as we use to be and I don't know where the breakdown happened.

    Is she seeing any of my inconsistencies? Maybe she knows that someone else is on my mind. Either way, we both have issues with each other and my biggest one at this moment is to find out how in the hell she got a car. "Olivia, before you walk out of this damn house I need to know where you got money from to get a car? Who helped you?" Before she exits, she stares at me with a smirk on her face and doesn't respond. "Who in the fuck bought you a car Olivia? Was it Alexander? Is that where you're going?"

Time stood still in those moments of her glaring at me, my temperature rises and she says, "The least of your worries is Alexander, Kayne. You can trust me on that." She walks out, closing the door behind her. I rush to the door, look outside to see what car she was headed to and I'll be damned if she didn't get into a Range Rover. From the door I could see her looking in my direction. She gets on her cell phone, shakes her head and drives off.

Furious, I stand there and watch her drive away. I want to follow her but I'm torn, one part of me doesn't want to know if she is still dealing with Alexander and the other doesn't give a damn. I have other interests because in Jasmine and my new money machine, *The Wild Card.*

As I look at her tail lights disappear into the night, I notice another car pull up and stops in my view. The passenger side window rolls down and I see someone staring at me. I am struggling to take a second look. Oh SHIT!!! I see it's the same car that was following me on the motherfucking freeway. It's Alexander and he knows where the hell I live. I run out to the street to but as I approach it, it speeds off into the night. He would have never known where I lived if Olivia hadn't told him. I can't believe she did this to me. I don't want to believe she had him around while I was gone. One thing is for sure, shit is about to get real. This fool needs to be taken care of because he obviously doesn't give a shit about boundaries.

He wants Olivia and again he is showing me that he will risk his own life to get her back. While walking back to my house I get an email alert of my phone. I open it up and notice it's an invite from The Congressman. He's having a huge dinner gala at the Beverly Hills Hilton and I'm still on his guest list. What a coincidence that I just received this after I had just manhandled his wife. This should be interesting.

CHAPTER 10
MEET THE CONGRESSMAN

A few weeks have passed and Olivia and I have been coexisting. I haven't asked her anymore questions about the money she *borrowed from* my account and she didn't ask me anything about my whereabouts when I left for a couple of days.

She repaid me all of my money back and explained that the truck she was driving was her girlfriend's vehicle that was going to be out of the country for a while. She was asked to take care of it while her friend was away. I don't know how she got that money back so fast and truthfully, I really didn't care. She has her secrets and I have mine. If we remain respectful about it, our indiscretions shall never cross paths.

It was the evening of the gala; a beautiful Saturday night filled with stars thrown across the Los Angeles sky. The invite allowed me to bring a guest so earlier that week I purchased Olivia a beautiful gown for the evening. It was a black strapless Christian Dior Resort Gown that complimented her shapely body; she looked magnificent in it. I was her compliment in my Christian Dior Parisian tuxedo that hugged my fit body like a glove. I must admit we look good together and I can't wait to show up at the Congressman's ball. Truthfully, my reasons for bringing Olivia is to keep me honest because I knew if I had the chance to do something I shouldn't do, if money was involved I will most likely jump at the opportunity.

I'm sure many of my conquests are going to be in the building and who knows there may be some more potential clientele that may need my services. It is my intention to make a good amount of money so that I can stop living the paid for play lifestyle and settle down and start a family with Olivia. I have been trying really hard not to step out but I had to meet with *The Wild Card* on many occasions following our initial meeting. She has paid liberally for my time so financially I was doing well; she kept my bank account healthy.

This woman's appetite is insatiable. While waiting for Olivia my mind drifted. I began reminiscing about another meeting we had. She didn't have much time to spare on one specific day because she was meeting her husband for lunch. She swore to me that if she didn't get to feel my dick deep inside of her, her pussy would be very sad. Now I couldn't allow her pussy to be sad on my account. Once she told me how much she would pay for the very brief encounter, I had no problem fucking her in the back of her BMW 800 series in the middle of the afternoon in the parking lot at the West Hills Shopping Center. We steamed up the windows pretty good that day but thinking back, I could have sworn I saw someone looking through the windows at one point. Nevertheless, I was fucking her so good that I wasn't about to stop the show for whomever was watching that day.

Olivia comes from the bedroom dressed in her designer gown, heels and clutch; she looks outstanding. "Damn, you look absolutely amazing baby." She gives me a twirl and pokes her bubble ass out for me to palm it. "You like dahhhhhhling?" Nodding my head yes. "I Lovvvvvvve it." I grab her and adorn her with a kiss. "Are you ready baby?" She checks her hair and make-up in the foyer as we head to the door.

Traffic is showing us mercy on this Saturday evening; we are able to drive across the city without any traffic problems. *Najee* is providing the soundtrack along our path toward Beverly Hills and my woman and I are enjoying our time together. "Kayne, these are the moments I love the most. I feel like we can conquer the world together. I truly hope we can and be able to put all of our past behind us and live the rest of our lives together."

Hearing her say this makes me feel renewed because I was still not feeling sure about her and her contact with Alexander. I guess I still haven't really gotten over that. Not to mention some other things that I have heard that just don't add up. However, I know I need to respond accordingly so that the night won't be flawed with attitude and negative emotions.

"I agree Olivia." I'm sure I could have said more but I didn't and she didn't ride me on it. We continued to listen to the smooth jazz until we pull up to the hotel.

As we are walking into the Ballroom of the party Olivia and I are notice that the crowd is filled with people from all walks of life; Senators, Governors, Elected Officials and Entertainers. They are all hob knobbing with each other before the festivities begin. We are walking around the room meeting and greeting different people. All around me I notice familiar faces in the crowd but something was different with these faces.

On this particular evening, these faces are doing their best not to make eye contact with me because they are with their significant others. I have already counted ten women who I have serviced. Some of them give me a sly smile or wink or nod. The Master of Ceremony gets our attention and everyone heads to their seats.

On our way to our seats, I notice that Regina is making a beeline in our direction. "Lord, I'm hoping this woman will have some discretion about herself. I hope she realizes that my woman is here with me and doesn't blow my cover." Regina is coming towards our table, I turn to Liv and say, "Babe that is Regina, the Congressman's wife, I met her at his last engagement. She is a very nice woman." Olivia smiles and waits as she approaches our table.

"Hello Kayne, how are you doing? It has been a while since I've seen you. How have you been?" I stand to give her a hug and respond. "I'm well; it has been a while since we've seen one another. I've been hanging in there, doing the best I can, you know how it is." This was my attempt at an innocent conversation, not to give anything away but Regina had something different on her mind.

"I surely do know how it is Kayne. From the looks of it, it seems like you are doing rather well." She draws in and gives me a hug that was much longer than usual and ends it with a quick kiss on my lips. She walks away without saying a word or even acknowledging Olivia. "What the fuck was that? I know that bitch see me sitting here?" I'm at a loss for words. I sit back down to the table puzzled. Olivia is not happy; her anger is written all over her face. "Why did you let her kiss you?" "So that what you do now, let random women kiss you on the lips? What the fuck is that about?" Shit, I wasn't expecting that. It happened so fast. It completely caught me off guard.

"Olivia, you saw it. I wasn't expecting that. I'm sure she was just being nice and working the room. Don't let it get to you babe." Fuming from my poor explanation, Olivia gets up from the table. She murmurs, "I have to use the restroom, I'll be back. Can you make sure that no there bitches come over here and disrespects me while I'm gone, can you fucking do that for me?" All I could do was look at her and shake my damn head.

I'm sitting at my table thinking about all the money I have made, watching all of the women I have I've fucked, prance around the room and all I can do is shake my head in awe. I can't believe that all of these well to do women are dissatisfied at home. Their souls are in shambles because they lack good dick at home. I could have easily made the acquaintances of new inquiries that have that look in their eye but I refuse to be on the hunt. I just look away to send them the message that I am not interested.

I'm going to be still and not allow my manhood to get the best of this great evening, plus, it's too close for comfort and the night has already given me an unexpected wrinkle with Regina's antics so I'll just sit here like the good guy and wait on my Olivia to return.

On Olivia's way back from the restroom

While coming out of the restroom, a well –dressed gentleman who could easily been my father approaches me. "Olivia is that you?" I stop in my tracks like I have just saw a ghost. I hesitate.

"Olivia, I never thought I'd see you again, it's been a very long time but I've never forgotten you; it's me Walter." Still in shock by who is front of me, I find the strength to respond to him because I remember who he is now. "Yes, I remember you. Oh my god what are you doing here? I haven't seen you since our….and he immediately cuts me off before I could finish my sentence. He reaches into his pocket and gives me his card.

"I really don't have time to talk but I really would like to catch up with you and possibly do business again if you know what I mean." I take the card and put it deep down in my purse. Before he walks off I stop him.

"Walter, those days are over. I don't have to do that anymore and I'm in a committed relationship." His smile turns into a scowl. He didn't seem to appreciate what I said. He grabs my arm and brings me close to him.

"Listen to me; you must have forgotten what happened between us. Have you forgotten Olivia?" I don't respond but you can see I'm visibly shaken by what he said. "Yes, you fucking remember so don't you stand here and give me that self-righteous shit. You were a fucking whore when I met you and you got a lot of money out of me. You were pregnant with my baby. You remember that? The baby you killed without telling me. I'm sure you don't want that type of information to get out to your guy do you. You did a pretty good job disappearing from your reality but I know the whole truth. Now you have my card and I'm expecting you to call me so that we can pick up where we left off. If I remember correctly, you had some of the best pussy and head any John could pay for right?"

He reaches into his pocket and pulls out a big wad of cash and stuffs it in my clutch. "Here's my retainer. Be available when I call you" and he walks away leaving me in state of shock. I gather myself before I head back to Kayne.

Back to Kayne

I see Olivia walking back from the restroom and she doesn't look to right. "Babe are you ok? You don't look well at all?" She sits down without looking at me. "Babe, what's wrong? Did something happen?"

I turn to see what is going on at the podium. I see security ushering the Congressman on to the stage. The speaker gets up to the mic.

"Hello everyone and welcome to the 15th Annual Congressman's Gala. This is a very special year. We are celebrating the Anniversary of our Congressman and his wife. Everyone please stand and give a round of applause for Congressman Walter and Regina Daniels."

Everyone stands and applauds except for Olivia who remained seated. She didn't even flinch. I know something is definitely wrong because she looks like she has seen a ghost. The night goes on, I try probing her for answers but she sits stoic, revealing nothing. After several attempts to get Olivia to come out of her funk I decided that maybe we should leave.

The gala was fantastic especially because I was able to keep my composure in a room of powerful women who could be on my list. I even managed to stay out of sight of Regina and the Congressman for the rest of the night. It was close to eleven and we both we were ready to go.

As we head toward the door, security interrupts us and urges me to follow them. I didn't know what this was about but I was curious to find out what the hell they wanted with me. "How can I help you?" There was three of them but only the tall one spoke. "The Congressman would like to speak with you."

Oh shit, what in the fuck does this man want to say to me? Does he know about me and his wife?" I look at Olivia and now her face is as white as a sheet. "Kayne I'm really tired, can we just go home right now?"

She grabs my hand and tries to pull me away but security insisted that I come with them and that Olivia wait for me. "Ok, I'll go and meet with him but I can't be long, my lady is not feeling well."

I give Liv a kiss and hand her the car keys so that she could wait in the car. "I won't be long baby." She snatches my keys and walks away; I proceed in the direction of the security guards to a hotel room off to the right of the ball room. They lead me to the door and walk away.

I'm having a *'What the Hell'* moment because I have no idea what is about to happen. The door opens and it's the Congressman. "Come on in and have a seat."

I walk in the door but I'm cautious as hell because I don't have a clue to why he would want to see me unless he knows something but am going to play it cool until he makes a move. "I'm not sure why you would want to see me Congressman Daniels so forgive me if I seem a bit on edge by this request." He grabs a cigar from his desk and lights it. He is very meticulous with his movements precise in his responses.

He takes a puff and fills the room with smoke. "Your name is Kayne right?" I'm sure he meets hundreds of people in his line of business and I am even more positive that his handlers take care of his guest list for his engagements so how in the hell does this man know my name?

"You are correct, I'm Kayne. What is this about?" He takes another puff of his cigar. "The word is out about you and from what I hear you are very good at what you do; I'm interested in spending some money for your services." There must be some confusion; I know this motherfucker is not asking me what I think he is asking me. I get up out of my seat to leave because if this goes any farther the Congressman and I will be having a problem that requires correction.

"I think you have me mistaken. I'm not into that. This is Los Angeles, I'm sure you will be able to find what you are looking for elsewhere." The Congressman has a puzzled look on his face like he has been completely offended by my response. He puts out his cigar in a nearby ashtray and stands. "What do you mean there are others I can find. Is my money not good enough for your services?"

This motherfucker is very insistent and not understanding the fact that I'm not interested in what he is suggesting so maybe I need to respond more aggressively so that he will have no problems comprehending my stance.

"Listen man, I'm not gay, so you keep your fucking money. I don't know why you even thought that this shit was a possibility!" The Congressman lets out a hearty laugh and responds.

"Man, I'm not gay!!!! I'm a heterosexual man just like you who loves pussy brother so relax. I heard you use to work for the best marketing firm in the city and you left to start your own business. Shit, I wanted to hire you to do some Strategic Marketing for me and I was willing to pay you well for your services."

Whew, I'm relieved because I thought I was going to have to beat this man's ass in this room tonight. I'm still very puzzled though, how does he know this information about me. I'm not even close to being in his circle of associates so why me? I know damn well he has the resources to get the best that money could buy but he said he would pay me well so I'm going to sit my ass back down and listen to his spiel. I am also interested to know if this is about his wife.

"Yes, I worked for Marketing Enterprises and did very well for them but it was time for me to get out and do my own thing. So tell me what do you need and what are you willing to pay?" We go over all of the details and what he is asking me to do for him seems very simple. So simple he could really do it himself but he says that his time won't allow him to do so.

"So are you interested?" The work wasn't the problem and it shouldn't take me no time to complete but my curiosity still is wondering why me? "Yes, I'm interested but I have to ask you. Of all the contacts you have why would you choose me? I mean I'm pretty good at this kind of work but I don't have the years of experience as others in this line of business."

He reaches back in the same drawer that he got his cigar from and pulls out an envelope. He offers it to me. "Yes, I could ask anyone to help me do this but I'm asking you. Here is your first payment. I'm sure that's enough. I'll have my people call you with other pertinent information." I look into the envelope and I see a band of $100 dollar bills. "That's 10K and there's more where that came from.

This is going to be a hush assignment so keep this close to the vest." I nodded ok and proceeded to write my number down. "There will be no need for that; I have your contact information. I'll call you." He shakes my hand and walks out of the room leaving me there alone.

I'm sure there is more to this but I'm on a mission to get as much cash saved up as I can so that I can leave the life I'm living on the clock and retire in the islands. If he gave up 10K like that I can only imagine how much more he could produce. His wife is also filtering money to me so I'm bound to make more from this transaction but I have to be careful he doesn't find out that his wife is paying for a little extra on the side.

If he knew already he would have mentioned it or confronted me so I'm going to walk out of here thinking that this coincidence is just a good opportunity to make some money. I head back to the car to meet Olivia who has been waiting for me for close to an hour. I open the door and see that she is pissed.

"What in the fuck took you so long? Why did he want to see you Kayne? What did he say to you?" She was very insistent in getting an answer and her eyes displayed worry. "He really didn't want anything Olivia. He just likes to meet his guest that attends his soiree. It was just my turn and of course with those Politicians they ask for a donation of some sort, that's all. Why do you seem so testy?"

She did not utter another word for the remainder of the evening. She lays her head back on the seat, closes her eyes as we head toward the freeway to go home. Approaching the east exit, I see a car exiting on the opposite side blazing their bright headlights. It gets my attention because it's blinding me so I flick my lights to let them know their bright lights are on.

I look closer when the car passes me so that I can give the driver eye contact and I notice the car looks familiar. In fact, it is very familiar. It was Alexander and he was headed toward the hotel that we just left. What in the hell is this? I look over to see if Olivia witnesses what I just saw but her eyes are still shut. I'm grinding my teeth because every part of my boiling blood wants to make a U-turn and go back to the hotel but my common sense tells me to leave this night alone and go home. And that's exactly what I did.

CHAPTER 11

JASMINE AND OLIVIA CROSS PATHS

A few weeks have passed since the Congressman's gala and things have been touchy between Olivia and me. I have done my best to work out the tension between us but it's just not the same.

We have been like two ships passing in the night since she has transportation. Now she has been leaving the house anytime she wants. I don't even question her anymore because I'm doing the same thing. I have met with Regina a few more times since the last encounter and I've been collecting big for it. My bank account is filling up fast and I'm doing it without having to spread myself paper thin.

I have even done some marketing work for the Congressman through email which still seems weird to me. Yes, all of this is pretty damn scandalous but why should I give a damn? Regina obviously has access to the money, the need for my dick and is clueless about me doing some marketing for her husband which is how I want to keep it.

Jasmine has been reaching out to me in the past few weeks through text messages and emails. She says she's planning a return trip to California but she didn't reveal when. Every time I ask her she replies, "I want to surprise you Kayne." Little does she know I hate surprises. However, today I will attempt to make some time for Olivia and see if we can iron out some of the wrinkles that need to be taken care of. I go to the bedroom where she is and I sit at the foot of the bed. "How are you doing today Liv?" She pulls the cover up on her chest before she responds. "I'm fine, how are you?" I see she is in mood to talk so I get comfortable and lay beside her. "Things have been kind of awkward between us lately and I just want to clear the air. I want to get back to the old us again if that is alright with you?" She looks at me and gives me a kiss. This is definitely not the response I expected. I expected more resistance but I'm guessing she is tired of the entire melee too so I kiss her back.

"That's fine with me baby but tell me something, why did the Congressman really want to see you at the party that night?" I thought I told her my answer when she asked before but I'll entertain the question again to keep peace. "He just wanted to personally meet some of his donors and thank them for their generosity.

It was a very simple meeting. Why are you so interested in knowing what we talked about? Since we are talking about that night, what happened with you when you went to the bathroom? You looked like you had seen a ghost." She pauses and takes a deep breath before she speaks. "Nothing was wrong Kayne. I just didn't feel well afterwards. Maybe it was something I had eaten that didn't agree with my stomach that's all."

I look at her because her answer didn't seem plausible to me. I know there has to be something else that moved her that night. She may not want to tell me today and that's fine I guess but I'm sure it will eventually reveal itself sooner or later as that is how my life goes when it comes to the affairs of the heart.

We are having a good conversation and even got a quickie in to take the edge off; we both were satisfied. "Baby do you want to take a shower with me?" Still in a semi-coma from the pleasurable make-up sex, she shakes her head no and pulls the cover over her entire body. I get out of the bed and head to the shower to clean-up because later tonight I have an engagement to fulfill.

Yes, I know I said I wasn't going back on the clock but there was a Chronicle I needed to satisfy. This millionaire Jane has sent me a picture and messages for weeks proclaiming her much needed desires to have me stating she travels to Los Angeles frequently. Jane has long money and I want some of it.

Meanwhile back in the bedroom

I'm lying in bed falling in and out of sleep. After a few minutes of me dosing off, I hear a buzz. I partially open my eyes to see where the buzz is coming from but I close immediately and try to go back to sleep thinking I am dreaming. Buzzzz! Buzzzz! I hear it again and this time, it wakes me. I get up and look around and notice its Kayne's cell phone notification that he is receiving text messages.

I look to make sure Kayne is still in the shower because I don't want to get caught doing what I'm about to do. I creep out of the bed to locate his phone. I pick it up and check it. Usually Kayne has his screen locked but today he was slipping. I close my eyes and say a quick prayer, "Please don't let this be not bull****."

I swipe the screen to read the messages and I see they are from a woman named Jasmine. What in the fuck is this shit and why is she texting Kayne? I scroll down and read the messages while still keeping a close ear on the shower to make sure that Kayne wasn't getting out. The water is still running, so I read further.

Hello Kayne my love, I have missed you since our last time together and I'm longing for you now. I told you that I was going to surprise you when I return to Los Angeles. Well guess what? I'm here my love. I want to see you and spend time with you again, real soon. I'll be staying at the Sofitel, room number #212. I'm here now and I will be waiting for you. Can't wait to taste and feel you again. I hope you have made a decision about you and me and our future. It's time to come home to Jamaica.

I hear Kayne turning off the water so quickly I grab a pen and piece of paper, write down Jasmine's number, hotel information and replace the phone where I found it before he comes out of the bathroom. I get back under the cover and pretend like I'm just waking up from my cat nap.

"Hey baby, are you getting ready to go somewhere?" Standing in the bathroom doorway, drying off and applying essential oils to my skin I say, "Yes, I have to go and meet this realtor about this spot I've been looking at. It's time to upgrade our living arrangement and move to a more exclusive area."

She has no idea that I'm really serious about what I just said because that motherfucker Alexander knows where we live and the other part of it is actually the lies

I've become accustomed to telling her so that I could get out to make this money.

"Ok baby, well go ahead and handle your business. I think I'm going to just stay in tonight and watch some movies. Take your time and don't worry about rushing back home, I'll be fine just relaxing." Now this was a pleasant surprise to hear those words coming from her mouth. Truthfully, it was a shock because she would always want to know when I would be returning or where in the hell I was going but today she gave me no resistance so I just rolled with it.

"Sounds like a plan baby; I'll give you a call before I come home and pick you up something to eat." She gives me a smile and says, "That sounds good. See you later." I proceed to get dressed without a worry in the world. I go over to the counter where my phone has remained untouched and place it in my jacket. I go over to give Olivia a kiss before I leave. She grabs my waist and begins to unzip my pants. "Let me take the edge off of you before you go, I promise you it won't take long and you can have something on your mind to make you want to hurry back home."

I have no problem with what Olivia is suggesting so I pull my tool out and she begins to give me a nice polish while I watch her work my perspective. Olivia has this thing that she does with her tongue in the slit on head that drove me wild. After five good minutes of her drowning my manhood with her saliva and the flickering her tongue on my head she would also grab my full balls and massage them.

She knew I loved that shit and it made my dick rock hard. Before I could firmly plant one of my legs on the bed so that she could get a better angle to get my entire dick in her mouth I let out a load that flooded her mouth. I watched it ooze from between her lips as she smiled up at me.

She wipes her mouth of any evidence of my excitement and says, "Now go to your meeting baby." I go and wipe myself down before I leave the house. I shake my head in disbelief because no matter what has happened between me and Liv she still knows how to smooth things over just right. She's still a beast in her own way. "See you later on tonight Liv." I leave the house on the clock and when I return I'll be a couple of grand richer.

Olivia's Words Now

He closes the front door, I jump out of bed and head to the window to watch him drive off. He can stay out all night as far as I'm concerned because I'm going to this hotel to see who this bitch Jasmine is and why she is texting my man.

It didn't take me long to throw on something that I could move around in just in case this woman wants to see if I'm about that life. I get dressed and I'm out the door. Walking to my truck, I see a car blinking their bright lights in my direction. It seems strange but I continued to car.

I'm assuming they are trying to get my attention but I'm not interested in being hit on right now so I ignore what I think are advances. I get in the truck, look into my rearview mirror to drive off and that car that was flickering the headlights is now parked behind me. I don't know who the hell this is because the car is unfamiliar to me. I get out of the truck to see who this was and why they were blocking me in. I got closer the face behind the wheel starts to look familiar.

Fuck me!!!!!! It's Alexander! How in the hell did he find out where we lived? Kayne cannot know this, I need to find out what is going on so I walk over to the driver's side and ask him to let his window down. "What are you doing here Alexander?!! You have to leave now!" He just looks at me and doesn't say a word, but revs his engine.

For some reason I'm not the least bit scared of him right now. Maybe it's because a part of me is afraid that if Kayne came back home he would see Alexander here at his house and that would be it for us because for damn sure he would think that I led Alexander here.

"How in the hell did you find me Alexander, you need to leave right now and never come back or ill call the police." Alexander is not fazed by my words and he remains silent but you could see the anger in his eyes.

"Bitch you should have never left me. I'm not going to fuck with you now. It's going to be a very slow process for you Olivia. I'm going to make sure that Kayne knows all about your fucked up past and why you ain't shit. Just know now that I can touch you whenever I want to." He backs up, peels off and speeds away leaving me looking at his tail lights.

What did I do to deserve this treatment? This man will not stop in his promise to destroy me and the possibility of me having a life with someone else. I walk back to my vehicle and get in because I still have to deal with this situation with this Jasmine chick.

I put the address in the navigation and I head to the Sofitel to meet my rival. As I pull up to the hotel I'm having some conflicting feelings. I'm still shaken at the fact that Alexander knows where I live, that's some scary shit because I know what he is capable of. Then there's this other woman who obviously has a past with Kayne.

How can all of this be happening when we are trying to make our relationship work? I can't lose Kayne, not now. We have gone thru so much already and I'm not about to lose him to another woman. If we have to leave this LA to survive I will be willing to do so but I refuse to let Alexander or this Jasmine bitch destroy what I know I could have with the love with my life in spite of the bullshit we have gone through. I get to the hotel and park. I don't know what is about to go down but tonight shit is about to hit the fan.

With butterflies in my stomach and anger in my heart, I head to the room. I hesitate before knocking on the door to gain my composure. I'm still unsure about this move I'm about to make but I'm prepared to fight for my man. I will do whatever it takes to protect our relationship.

Here I am in front of room #212. I'm about to get the answers to the questions that are pulling at my heart strings. I knock twice and wait, still nothing. I knock harder this time and wait for a response. Nothing. My heart is racing.

I don't know what to do. Should I leave a note or sit right here in front of this door until she comes back? Should I just leave and save myself from the answers that I'm really afraid to hear?"

After a minute or so of knocking and no answer, I knock one last time and she responds. "Is that you Kayne? I'm coming baby." So she just knew that Kayne was going to come. Well you are about to be surprised Ms. Jasmine.

She opens the door and immediately her smile turns into a look of concern. "I'm sorry but you must have the wrong room." She proceeds to close the door but not before I stick my foot in opening to prevent her from closing it.

"I'm sure you were expecting someone else but you got me. You were expecting Kayne I'm assuming?" Jasmine gives me a look like how would I know this information.

"How do you know Kayne and why are you here?" We both are curious in each other's relationship with Kayne; she can see it on my face, so she opens the door and motions for me to come inside.

I walk in the room and notice that she is playing soft music and has a very nice black lace Alexandra Popa and Javier Suarez Bordelle laid across the bed. This bitch is jazzy and she has some freaky intentions for tonight. More than talk was going to go on in this room if Kayne would have shown up. I sit down and she turns off the music.

"Excuse me but I didn't get your name and why you are here?" I reposition myself in the chair and take in the ambiance. She has created a welcoming, very sensual environment for her and Kayne.

"I'm Olivia. I'm Kayne's fiancé; we live together. I saw your text about you being in town and wanting to see him and I just had to know who you were."

She goes to sit in the opposite chair across from me and speaks in a dialect that was familiar. Obviously she is Jamaican like Kayne. "Yuh bey his fiancé yuh say. Him nevah spoke bout cha to meh nevah."

Now sometimes I can't understand some of the shit Kayne says when he speaks patois but I understood everything this bitch was saying. Her malice laced response pissed me the fuck off so in my best attempt to respond back in their native language I told her ass, 'Well him nevah spoke bout cho ass eeeeeeether so I guess this is where we need to get acquainted because these text messages will cease after tonight, believe that! Hear me loud and clear, we are in love and plan to get married someday real soon." She smiles like I have cracked a fucking joke.

"Listen to me closely, we just met and I don't know anything about you. Kayne has never spoken your name so your emphasis on being in love and thoughts of getting married means nothing to me. When I was here last time, I saw no signs that he was in love with you."

The nerve of this pretty Jamaican bitch talking down to me like I was a low class whore. "What exactly do you mean? Kayne and I have a long history and I'm sure whatever little tryst you may have had with him was something you paid for. I hope that you enjoyed it too because that was the last time you will even feel the curve of his dick again!"

She pulls out her cell phone, scrolls through her text messages and lets me read what she felt I needed to see. She politely hands me her phone.

"Here, you read all you want and yuh tell me if dat man is in love with yuh."

Jasmine strolls into the bathroom cocky as hell like she just laid out her last spade and ran a Boston on my ass.

With a look of disgust on my face, I start scrolling and reading. I notice that these text messages between them have been going on since his last trip back to Jamaica.

"*I love you….. I miss you…. I need to feel you…… Some of the best pussy I've ever had….. Can't wait to spend more time with you….. We will be together, you are such a beautiful woman………*

The text went on and on about how much he was into her. My heart sunk; I actually felt my stomach doing summersaults after reading all of this.

There was nothing even spoken about me in those text and it's obvious that he does care for her. I'm not going to allow her to see my emotions though. Her ass needs to know emphatically that her chances of getting my man are next to know. That bitch will have a fight on her hands if thinks I'm going to just lay down and let her move right in on Kayne. She comes back from the bathroom dressed and sits down. I hand her back her phone.

"So as you can plainly see Kayne is very much available and his interests lie elsewhere. So this is what I think you should do. I think you should get your pathetic little ass up and get the fuck out of here. The nerve of you intercepting a text that wasn't meant for you. That is clear indication of your immaturity, insecurities and proves you cannot be trusted. No real man would put up with a woman who displays this type of behavior. That is what yuh get from being so damn nosey. Well you got your answers. He will make that choice, not you. You can leave now."

Jasmine goes to the door and opens it. This bitch may be pretty and looks like she has class but there is something about her. Although I want to just jump on her ass like a wild alley cat because of the way she is talking to me I'm going to refrain because I need to find out more about what is going on between them, so I get up and head toward the door.

"This is not over Jasmine not the least. I will tell you one time, one time ONLY, STAY AWAY from Kayne. He is mine and we will be together forever. So please tread carefully because I'm not an easy win, Bitch!"

As I'm head out the door Jasmine gets one last jab in before our impromptu meeting ends.

"Olivia, he's a Jamaican man and they always come home….remember that!" She slams the door.

My heart is broken into a million pieces from what I just found out. I would have never guessed that another woman has Kayne's heart like this. Do I ask him about her? If I do he will know that I checked his phone and meet with her?

Will he find out from her if he goes to see her? I can't let that happen and I will find out what I need to without giving myself away.

Is this the Karma that I get from the pain that I've caused him? Jasmine is a very pretty woman and I could see why Kayne would be attracted to her.

She is also from Jamaica. I want to confront him about her because he has been keeping this a secret and we agreed that we were going to be honest with each other. Fuck!!!! I can't let her stay around. She cannot have Kayne.

We will get married no matter how we get there. We will be walking down the aisle……….TOGETHER. Jasmine will be a distant memory.

CHAPTER 12

MILLIONAIRE JANE CHRONICLE

I knock on the suite's door in hopes that the woman I saw in the picture was going to be the same woman who opens this door. A few seconds pass and still no answer so I knock again.

Suddenly, I hear a voice, "Come in Kayne." I open the door and slowly walk in the room. Her accent was thick and I knew she had money because this suite was immaculate.

It had a glass waterfalls built inside the walls of the room that connected to a whirlpool Jacuzzi that sat in the middle of the floor. The bed was the size of two Cali Kings covered with some of the finest silk sheets ever made.

Covering this play pen was the whitest, plush fur comforter that alone must have cost over ten grand itself. The room was slightly cold and dimmed while purple mood lights highlighted different areas on the bed.

I walk closer to the bed and I notice a body standing in the dark corner of the room. Her silhouette suggests that she is shaped like a fine winding country road. Everything was firm and as she walked closer to me where the lights were brighter I noticed that she was indeed the woman on the pics; she was absolutely beautiful.

"I've been sending you emails for months Kayne and there has been no response. Were you dissatisfied with the pictures I sent you?" My mouth wanted to say what my mind was thinking…"You fucking right I liked them and I'm about to tear your pussy apart" but I decided to be a bit more diplomatic.

"I've just been so busy that I didn't have time to get to my inquiries until just recently. I am impressed nonetheless." She walks by me and grabs my hand and heads toward the open bay window overlooking the city. "It's a beautiful night in Los Angeles isn't it? Not a cloud in the sky.

"You know I made a special trip especially to see you. I was hoping that your research of me would interest you a bit more than just the pictures." She grabs my hands and pulls me closer as we overlook the city and take the scene. I can smell her perfume on the back of her neck as it swirls in the night air. I feel the warmth our bodies create as I embrace her.

"Yes, I did some research on you; I found out that you are indeed a very wealthy Austrian business woman who made much of her money from tourism and hospitality. You personally own five of the ten most profitable resorts in your country as well as the main developer of a literacy program that was sold to all the schools to boost tertiary education."

Yes, I did my homework on this woman. She hit me with that *I'm a Millionaire* shit in her emails so I wanted to see exactly if it was true and VERY TRUE indeed.

"You missed something Kayne, I'm not very wealthy; I'm extremely wealthy and I expect to spend some good money on the best dick my Austrian pussy can get in America."

She turns to me and grabs my face to kiss her. Her mouth was warm and her lips were very soft. My dick has awaken and knows he is about to get some work in tonight but I don't unleash him yet. I want her to get me to the point where my dick is fighting to get out of my pants to fuck her.

"Your tongue is good Kayne and your full sexy lips are like soft fluffy pillows, I'll bet you can eat some good pussy." I love the fact that this Austrian woman can turn me on with her words with her sexy ass accent.

"You will soon find out," as I put my hands down her tight panties. "Ahhhhh, your hands and fingers are strong. Go deeper Kayne." I stick two fingers inside of her wet hairless pussy and her head tilts back, her moaning continues.

She turns her back to me again and says, "Finger me from the back using your whole hand Kayne." She bends over and spreads her legs wide and I proceed to stick my fingers one by one inside her hot spot until the middle of all of my fingers were inside of her.

This turned her on because she began to thrust against my hand, not flinching. "You like that love? How does that feel?" She grabs her own ass while bracing herself on the railing, her breast free to feel the evening breeze.

"Oh yes it feels so good Kayne. In my ass now, put your fingers in my asshole." This woman wasted no time in asking for what she wanted and I LOVED IT.

My dick is steadily growing and waiting for his chance to perform but not just yet. I'm feeling the pre-ejaculation begin to ooze from my head and my balls are beginning to throb. The cum in my balls is boiling now and she knows it. While I am fisting her wet asshole, she reaches back and squeezes my erect goodness.

When she felt my thick black snake uncoil itself in my loose fitting linen pants it was then that I forced her to accept the fact that what she had been accustomed too was just a rehearsal for the real thing.

I was the main attraction. She had merely been spending her time with opening acts. She doesn't know right off hand that she needs a backstage pass and my concerts always remain sold out. Even in Austria. Her money couldn't get access the kind of dick she was about to experience unless she got it from me and only me. From the look on her face she knew she was about to be indulging in a real performance and my instrument was a bass; it was going to go deep.

I am so turned on by fist fucking her ass, hearing her cry out and watching her body language that felt it was time to release the beast. I pull my thick headed manhood out of my pants, took the hand that I had been fingering her now wet, hot, dripping pussy and put my forefinger in my mouth.

I then took that same sin filled finger and rubbed the head of my thick red head and watched her just stare.

"I have never seen a cock that big before. They don't make them like that in my country. It was true what I heard about you." My dick was now standing at attention and she knew what that meant as I had no more words for her.

She knelt down to her knees on that balcony, put her long hair in a bun and sucked every inch that I had until my balls met her chin.

"Spit on my dick. Get it wet, I like it sloppy." And that she did, she spit in her hand and covered my dick and balls and made my tool look like a water slide and I proceed to fuck the back of her throat without caring if she choked or not.

Her throat felt so damn good and she didn't care how much I rammed it as she grabbed my ass and pulled me deeper into her mouth. After 15 minutes of a good throat fucking, water started to stream down her face from her icy blue eyes because the inches she took gave her no other fucking choice.

"Take me to the bed and give me your cock Kayne. I want you to give me the fuck of my life." I pick her naked body up from the balcony and take her to the plush bed that awaits us. I lay her down softly and then I get undressed.

While watching, she continues to finger herself and grind the sheets awaiting me to plow into her hole. She points over to the night stand where the condoms were and I lace my thickness with one.

"Open your legs wide for me." She does with no problem. I maneuver her so that I can get her in a scissor position and I straddle on leg while holding the other on my shoulder.

I take my dick and slowly push it inside of her while taking the opposite hand and sticking my finger in her ass because she loves that. "You feel so good Kayne. Your dick is so thick. It hurts but I won't tell you to stop. I want you to rip me apart Kayne!"

Why did she say that to me? Not only did it get me harder than before but it also made me throw caution to the wind and I fucked her senseless. She allowed me to have full range with her pussy and ass. Her body was letting off a sweet pheromone that filled the room and that was my aphrodisiac. Every time I went deep inside of her I pulled out some of Austria's richest cream.

After fucking her hard for an hour she turned and grabbed my dick and squeezed it until my head turn beet red. "Now what do you want to do with that?" She walked me over to the warm Jacuzzi that was in the middle of the suite and she bent over halfway on the stairs. "Fuck my ass now." Her pussy had been beaten so good that all of her juices had laced her tight asshole and gave it a shiny glow for my clear entrance and I gave her ass pleasure like she asked.

I took my time there with her because the damage I could have caused would not have been reversible.

"Now when you are about to cum Kayne, I want you to take off that condom and shoot your load on my asshole." I'm looking at this woman like I had just seen a rabbit with human feet. This shit was remarkable as they don't make them like this in America and I started stroking and stroking.

"Here it comes baby…Here it cums…Oh shit!!!!!" I pull off the condom and she spread her cheeks wide and I released my platinum juice all over her asshole and she just rubbed it in and enjoyed every drop of it.

"Yessssssssssssssssssssssssss, that's it. Let it all out Kayne!" and she continues to suck her fingers and then turns to clean the rest of that cum with her mouth.

This woman was a winner and by the time I left her suite I had earned a cool 12K and she even gave me five free week vouchers to all of her resorts in Austria if I ever wanted to vacation in her country. The millionaire Jane proved her worth tonight.

It is only ten o'clock when I left the hotel and I promised that I would pick up some food for Olivia. It's funny, I didn't even think about her while I was on the clock tonight. Maybe it was because this Jane was the bomb in bed and made me forget about reality or maybe I'm happier being a Cocksman. Time always tells the future. I head home now to Liv and I hope she is sleepy because I'm not even in the mood to fuck again tonight.

CHAPTER 13

HE WON'T GIVE UP ON HER

"I know where she lives. I've been to her house. I'm getting her back no matter what it will take and if I have to kill him, I will."

Shaking his head at what he has just heard from Alexander. "What is your fucking problem Alexander? She was a trick that we both picked up from off the streets and you went and fell in love with the bitch. You must have forgotten?"

"Don't call her that and yes I remember. So fucking what!!! Your past ain't pretty and neither is mine. I know a different side to Olivia. "While lighting up a cigar in his plush cigar room he says, "You know you have always been a sensitive motherfucker and now you have gone off the deep end. You never fall in love in with a whore. What is it about her anyway? Why did she leave your ass again?"

Anger is riding on Alexander's face as he sits down in a chair." I fucked up. I let my jealousy and anger get the best of me and she left with this playboy motherfucker. She has this dumb ass idea that she is in love with this gigolo and she has a future with him. I found some emails that she was sending him and I couldn't take it anymore.

I refuse to just let her cheat on me over and over again so I snapped and I............."You what? You put your hands on her like you have done with every woman who wanted to leave you because your ass is sensitive and jealous? When will you learn that you cannot force a woman to stay where she isn't happy?"

Not wanting to hear much more of this scolding because he has heard this all before, Alexander gets up and begins to walk out.

"Sit your ass down! That's your problem, you have no discipline. I've spent a lot of money getting your ass out of trouble and I'm sick of it. You fuck up this time, it's on you. I will not use my influence to get your ass out of trouble again. You are my brother and I love you but I will walk away from you like you never existed if you do anything stupid over that woman."

Alexander walks up on his brother and gets in his face. "You think because you have this prestige and money that you are better than me don't you? Again, you have a past too. You haven't always been the almighty "Congressman Walter" so give me a break with this uppity talk. You are talking all this stuff, tell me, what would you do if you found out that Regina was fucking over you and loving it?"

That must have hit a nerve with Walter because his calmness turns into anger. "Don't you come into my house disrespecting me and talking about my wife like that. Regina would never do that to me. Watch your mouth!!!" Smiling now, he sees that he has touched a nerve with Walter.

"What's wrong Walter? Is there something you want to discuss? Who is the sensitive one now brother?" Alexander goes and pulls out a picture out of his bag and shows it to Walter.

"This is him. This is the gigolo that came into my house and took Olivia from me. His name is Kayne. He is supposed to be this big time playboy that women all over the city are going crazy over. Olivia is in love with him and refuses to come back. You know I'm not going to let this happen and I will deal with him like I've dealt with the others. You remember the others right? The ones you helped your little brother get rid of never to be seen again because you knew special people in very low places?"

Walter grabs the picture and looks at it very closely and his suspicions were confirmed. That was definitely the same guy that he saw his wife with in the back seat in that parking lot that day he followed Regina. He needed to make sure that his suspicions were correct. He had heard Regina having conversations to her girlfriends about this Cocksman who was turning all of these women out and they would pay him top dollar for his services.

Walter hid his disappointment and anger from Alexander because he didn't want to reveal the same emotions he was telling his brother not to have.

"What's wrong Walter? Why are you quiet?" He gives the picture back to Alexander. "So that's the guy who Olivia is with now? Alexander nods his head yes.

"And you say you know where they live?" Alexander is now giving Walter a curious look as if to say why are you so interested now?

"Yeah I know where they live. You seem really interested; before you were telling me I was foolish."

Walter goes back to his seat and sits and re-lights his cigar. "You know Olivia was at the gala. She must have left before you got there."

Interested to find out more about Olivia being there he asks more questions. "Was she with him? Did you see her with him? And why was she there anyways, I know she wasn't on your guest list." Blowing smoke in the air, "I didn't see anyone with her and as far as I know she came alone. You damn right I didn't invite her so she had to have come with someone who was on my list." Deep down inside Walter knew who Olivia was with that night and he became more enraged at the fact that the man who had had sex with his wife was at his gala with a whore that he and his brother has slept with. The same whore he got pregnant who killed his baby because he made her for it would mess up his chances to run for Congress at the time.

Kayne was fucking both of the brothers over and just like that another enemy was confirmed. "Walter, I can't lose her to this clown and he's not going to get away with coming into my house and challenging me. As long as I'm breathing Kayne will have a problem with me.

She's hiding her past, I know it and if she keeps fucking with my emotions he will find out about his little Princess and all of the scandalous shit she did with me."

Walter is just standing there taking it all in because he has a different agenda. He has not told anyone his affiliation with Kayne and why he is keeping him close.

"You say you know where they live right?" Alexander takes notice at the look on his brother's face and replies. "Yes I do, why?" Walter goes to his desk and grabs his keys from the drawer and looks at Alexander.

"Let's go." Alexander doesn't know what the hell is going on at the moment but he is ready and willing to accommodate his brother on his request. It's close to midnight and the freeways are silent as they make their twenty mile trip. Behind the tinted windows of a Black 2015 Bentley Flying Spur they pull up and park.

"This is it. This is where they live." Walter gets out of the car and looks around. He doesn't speak any words, he just looks around. He notices a familiar truck that is parked outside the house. It's the same truck that he bought for Olivia years ago that she told him was stolen and never recovered.

You could see his anger beginning to cover his face with every thought of deceit from his wife and Olivia. By this time, Alexander has gone over to see what Walter is looking at.

"What's going on?" Walter begins to walk away with disgust on his face, "That truck looks very familiar to me and I don't like it. Do you know what Kayne drives?"

There were no more words spoken after that. It was almost like Alexander knew what his brother meant by it and from a side holster, he pulls out a silver plated 9mm and begins to light both vehicles up tires and all leaving behind two bullet riddled smoke filled vehicles that are now blaring their alarms.

They hurry back to the car to leave. As they begin to pull away they notice me from a distance running toward the moving car. They wait a bit longer but Alexander already knew who it was and gets out of the car and stands beside the door with his gun drawn by his side.

"Yeah you bitch, it's me. I ain't trying to hide!!" I can smell the gun powder in the air and knows this crazy motherfucker won't be playing fair tonight if he approached him carelessly.

"It's mighty feminine of you to come to a man's house and shoot up his vehicle! I hope you got a good hard on. And speaking of hard on, Olivia is waiting for me upstairs. Fuck it, you can shoot up all the cars. I still got what you want!"

This infuriates Alexander, throws the gun in the car and decided that he wants to teach me a lesson that he didn't get to teach me the first time we locked horns but I also hear a voice from inside the car.

"Get your ass back in this car and let's go now!" Alexander gives a pause just to stare me down and gets back in the car. The voice sounded very familiar to me and I began to run toward the driver's side to see who those words belonged too. As I got closer, the car begins to pull off with tinted windows now being raised and leaving me standing there wondering what the fuck is going on.

I go to survey the condition Alexander has left my car in. I also notice that Olivia's friend's truck has also been destroyed. Why in the hell would he do this to her truck? He doesn't even know who this belongs too.

With the smoke still filtering the air, I get inside my car to survey the damage I see that Olivia has come to see why the alarms were going off. As I begin to disconnect both batteries from the vehicle Olivia notices her truck.

"Who did this Kayne?!!!!! Oh my god what is going on?" I look at her because she has to have a good idea of who the culprit is. "You know Alexander knows where we live don't you?"

She looks at me like she has no clue why I am asking her that question. "No, I don't know that Kayne. How would he know that, I didn't tell him? I haven't been in contact with him. I wouldn't do that to us!" I just look at her. Alexander has been following me and somehow found his way to my part of town where he could touch us anytime he wanted.

This is definitely a sure sign that we have to move immediately but what's even more important about tonight was the voice I heard in the car.

She said there would be no limit to how far he would go to get her back. Well now I'm truly convinced. Alexander will never let her go.

CHAPTER 14

HE KNOWS..........

It has been a couple of weeks since the incident and I knew it was time to move. I had made enough money from a few of my engagements and it afforded me to be able to move to a condo in Century City and that's what Olivia and I did.

You could tell that our connection wasn't the same from that night but we still fought through in hopes that we could reconnect like old times. In all honesty I believe we both were living a lie but trying to force a love that wasn't meant to be but neither one of us was ready to concede to the truth.

Olivia had gone shopping today and I was home alone just relaxing. I was wondering why I hadn't heard from Jasmine in a while. She would have text or called me by now but there was nothing. I text her a few times but there was no response.

As I was going through old text messages I come across a few of Jasmine's messages that I didn't even knew existed. How in the hell did I miss this? She was in town a few weeks ago and was waiting on me to come see her. I never got a notification, hell I didn't even know that she was coming. Was this the surprise she had spoken of earlier? How did I miss these texts?

Something is not right but I have to get in touch with her to let her know that I was not trying to ignore her. I locate her number in my phone and call. There is no answer and it goes straight to voicemail.

I go back to the text and see that she gave the hotel and room number. Chances are she has already left the city but I have to make sure that she hasn't. I know that she thinks I've ignored her and that's far from the truth.

I've actually been missing her and wanting her more and more. She has me thinking about coming home to Jamaica and enjoying every sunset with her lying in my arms. I get up and begin to get dressed and my phone begins to ring. It's a blocked number. I usually don't answer blocked numbers but I was curious because it could be Jasmine returning my call from a private business line so I answer.

"Hello." There is no immediate response so I say hello again.

"Hello Kayne, this is Walter. Are you busy?" Shocked that I received this call today, I wanted to know what was on his mind. "I was about to head out for the day but I have a little time, what's up, do you need me to do some more marketing for you?" I'm assuming that's why he called.

"No, that marketing campaign is over. Thanks for all that you did but I won't need those services anymore. I need to talk to you face to face. Can you meet me at the Bonaventure in a half an hour? I'll accommodate you for your time?"

What in the fuck does this guy need to talk to me about if it's not concerning the business he hired me for? I was always worried if he ever found out about me and his wife and I'm thinking he knows more than he is letting on.

"Walter, I really don't have that much time. Can we try and schedule something another time?" He wasn't trying to hear that as he upped the ante.

"One thousand dollars will be waiting for when you get to the Bonaventure to pay for the inconvenience. "Meet me at the bar." and he hangs up. I don't know what could be so pressing but if he's willing to pay me a 1K to show up, I'll become interested in what he has to say.

Dressed and headed downstairs to get in my rental. I receive my keys from the valet and say hello to security and I drive toward downtown to meet Walter before I head over to see if Jasmine still is in town. It's a beautiful day and it couldn't be more perfect despite this surprise meeting.

I pull up to the hotel and give the valet my keys. I walk into the lobby and ask the doorman to point me in the direction to the bar and I head over to find a seat. I see that I have made it here before him and that's fine. I like to be settled in so that I can survey a situation especially when the shit seems suspicious to me and I patiently wait.

After about twenty- minutes of sitting and drinking a few glasses of cranberry juice there were no signs of Walter. I don't have time to waste like that so I decided to leave. Hell if he really wanted to discuss something with me he would have shown up. I pay my tab with the bartender and I begin to walk toward the valet.

My phone rings and it's from a private number again. This time I'm sure it's probably Walter calling so I answer. "Hello."

"Kayne, I'm sorry about the mix up. I'm here already but I'm upstairs in room #2201, Come on up. I have your money and an extra grand for me being late. I'll be waiting."

The money this man just throws around is crazy to me but if he is willing to pay it, I'll dance around with the devil for a little while.

I head to the elevator to go to the room and although I'm getting paid just to meet and talk I'm feeling real weary about this. As I get off the elevator on the twenty-second floor I stop for a minute to think this over.

Why did he change plans all of a sudden? Why couldn't he have asked me what he wanted to know over the phone? The majority of the business I had been doing for him was either by phone or through email; we rarely met so this was suspicious.

Nonetheless, I was still intrigued so I headed to the room. I knock on the door and I wait for him to answer. After a few minutes of me standing in the hallway looking around the door opens and it's Regina.

What in the fuck is going on?!! She has a worried look on her face and her eyes are filled with water. Awkward overcomes me now as this uncertainty has been confirmed.

Her eyes told me to turn around and leave immediately but Walter walked up behind her before I could turn away.

"Come in Kayne." I walk in and he shuts the door and locks it. Regina goes over to the other side of the room and sits quietly. She refuses to look my way; Walter just stands and looks to see what my response will be after seeing his wife in the room at the same time.

Walter goes to sit down. He offers me a seat in the middle of the room. "So why did you need to meet me Walter, what's going on here?"

Lighting his cigar, he takes a moment before he replies. He blows a big puff in the air and looks at me with a vile stare. He reaches in the drawer and pulls out an envelope and throws it to me.

"This will be your last payment Kayne." I'm assuming he is talking about the marketing job that he hired me for but it was still weird to me that he would bring this up in front of his wife because he told me not to mention our involvement ever.

"It has come to my attention that my wife has been spending my money without telling me what the fuck she was spending it on and this concerns me."

My mind is racing and the butterflies in my stomach have started to go crazy but I still attempt to play it cool and just listen to what he is saying.

"You see, Regina has a history of taking my hard earned money and using it for things she knows that I would never approve of but this latest expenditure really gets under my skin because of the level of deceit. Have you ever been deceived Kayne to the point where it's unforgivable?"

I look over and I see Regina's tears that were once welled up in the corners of her eyes are now rolling down the side of her face.

"Hey man, I don't know what's going on here but I don't think I need to be involved in this." And I get up to leave.

"Where do you think you are going Kayne? You aren't going any damn where. You are on the clock. You know what on the clock means don't you?"

Well now it has been verified. He knows that his wife has been stepping out on him. My mindset goes from a bit of cautiousness to survival mode now because he has a look on his face that doesn't say this is going to end well but something else got my attention.

His voice took me back to the night when Alexander shot up the vehicles. It was in the same tone that I heard. So I'm staring at him like is there more to this story.

"Who do you think you're talking too Walter? I'm not one of your fucking hired hands. You don't run anything over here. I can leave when I'm good and damn ready."

Obviously he had this shit all planned out because all of a sudden two armed men come from the bathroom and stand in front of the door.

"You do what you must do Kayne but I can assure you this, you make the wrong decision you and Olivia will pay a very high price for it and you can trust my word on that."

How in the hell does he know about Olivia and what does she have to do with this?

"What did you just say about Olivia?" Smoke is still filling the air from his cigar.

"That got your attention didn't it motherfucker. You're in love with that whore?"

Everything in me wants to go charge his ass and make him rescind that comment but there are three guns in this room all meant for me so my common sense keeps screaming at me to sit my ass down and just take it.

"I know who she is. I've known her for a very long time. We have a history together. A history she doesn't want you to know and it's amazing that now our paths have crossed like this."

He walks over to Regina and grabs her arm and her chair and places it next to me in the middle of the room.

"You do know Kayne, don't you Regina?" At this point she is in full flow of tears and I know she is afraid to answer that question so I jump in to bring some of the attention to me, "Why are you doing this man? This isn't right."

He comes over to me and looks me in my face, "Motherfucker what's not right is my fucking wife funneling thousands of dollars of my money and taking care of you, that's not right. What's not right is that I had all of her computers and phones hacked and I saw every text message and email that she has ever sent. She thought she was being slick by buying another phone. You weren't slick enough Regina!"

He looks at her with his fist clinched tight. "Yes, I seen everything you grimy Bitch!" as he turns back to me.

"What's not right is that I been having my wife followed for years because she has a habit of fucking over me and I tried to overlook some of it because of some of my past indiscretions but on this one unusually hot day I had to follow her myself. Regina felt she needed to take a ride and meet someone in a parking lot garage and fuck her paid boy toy in broad daylight in the back seat of a car that I bought for her. That's what's not right you pay for play gigolo."

The cat has just been let out of the bag and I was caught.

"Listen Walter, let's talk this out man. I can explain this."

You could see his handlers getting restless as they reached for their guns. I kept my eyes on them because I definitely would not want to be surprised by a gun to the back of my head. I am in a room with a man who just pretty much told me that he knows that I've been fucking his wife and there's nothing that I can do about it.

"There's nothing to explain Kayne. I know that my wife of 25 years and the mother of my 4 kids have been paying you to fuck her and that day where the both of you were in the back seat behind steamy foggy windows and you looked up and thought you saw someone watching? It was me and I should have bust the windows right then and killed the both of you but I didn't because I had to make sure and I was right all along. Regina, do you like fucking Kayne?" Was me providing for you not enough?"

She begins to dry her eyes as I could still hear her heart beating out of her chest. She looked at me with concern and I had no idea that she was going to say what she did and she let Walter have it.

"Walter, I love how Kayne fucks me. He does shit you could never do. I suck his dick like it's the last dick on earth and I swallow all of his juices. You think just because you have provided me with jewels, cars, trips and homes that I could overlook the countless women you have screwed over the years in my face. Yes Walter, I know about your shit too. I know about your secret trips and the different women in every state. Your private campaign fund and yes, I know about the bitch that you got pregnant."

Walter cannot believe what he is hearing right now because the tables are turning fast as he is listening to his wife deliver facts.

"Get that dumbass look off of your face. You think I didn't know? You thought you could just buy my memory and continue to disrespect me? Yes all of this is fucked up and Kayne I'm sorry that you have to be included in our dysfunction but Walter you haven't been right for a long time so stop with this shit right and let Kayne go. This is between you and me now."

Walter is furious with what he has just heard and I'm scared for what he looks like he is about to do to her.

"So you are going to sit up here and tell me how you like spending my money buying dick and expect me to be ok with that?"

"You asked and I told you the truth. You could never be Kayne Walter, your dick aint long enough to reach the depths that I have wanted you to hit for years."

That was last straw because he put down his cigar and slapped the shit out of Regina and knocked her out of the chair. I get up to help her back up and he pulls out his gun and points it at me.

"Let her ass stay where she is and you get back in this chair."

He picks up his wife and looks in her face.

"You know you have truly fucked up don't you? The disrespect you have just displayed will be dealt with and when I'm done with you, rest assured, you will have regretted ever answering the ad on THAT LIST. Yes you have been on THAT LIST for a while now. He is NOT the only pay for play dick you have had. I know Regina. I know your every move but you fell in love with this one."

With blood trickling from her lip she looks at Walter and gives him one more deadly blow.

"You are really a bitch to be hitting a woman. I'm your wife and the mother of your kids. Walter you better believe that there hasn't been a hole that Kayne didn't enter that I didn't love. You should take some lessons from him maybe that would have kept my ass home and by the way, I'm pregnant!"

Walter has had enough of her mouth and he motions to his handlers to get me out of the room.

"Kayne, we are done here. You stay away from my fucking wife from this point on but you will see me again, I promise that you will see me again. Now get the fuck out of here, your services will be no longer be needed!"

They open the door and push me out of it. I look back and give Regina one last look because I knew our business relationship had just ended.

I never condone any violence of a man putting his hands on a woman and somehow Walter will pay for that but for now I'm going get my ass far away from this drama as possible and head to where I should have gone in the first place. Please still be here Jasmine, I need you.

Back In The Room

"What in the hell you mean you are pregnant? We haven't been having sex Regina. You mean to tell me you have been having unprotected sex with that motherfucker?!" Regina just stares at him without saying a word and puts her head down because she knows he really doesn't want to hear that answer.

"Answer me dammit!!!" Still there are no words from Regina. Walter goes over to the phone and begins to dial. After a few seconds it is revealed who he is calling. "Alexander we need to talk. I think we have some business to tend too."

CHAPTER 15

JASMINE MAKES A STAND

I knew I was taking a chance on what could be a blank trip to the hotel. Weeks have passed and I know Jasmine should have already left but my desire and my heart is telling me that I need to see for myself.

I'm still dealing with the emotional realization that I just had a gun pointed to my head from the Congressman and his goons. That was a clear sign to me that I needed to clean up my act and get out of this life. I need to make a decision on what my future will be with Olivia or Jasmine because If I don't I'm afraid that something bad is going to happen to me.

My love for Olivia is revealing some horrible things about her that I didn't sign up for. There is more to her story that I'm continuously finding out and I don't know who she really is. Her history with Walter baffles me because I don't know how they could have come across each other. First there's Alexander and now Walter? What am I going to find out next about this woman? I don't know how much more I'm willing to take because the longer I stay around her the more my love is questioned.

Maybe we just need to move away from everyone who knows us and go somewhere where we could start a new life together and can't be found.

Well first I need to see if Jasmine is still here and where her mind is because she is the only one who could throw a monkey wrench in my program now. I can't seem to shake her from my mind.

I get to room #212 and I knock on the door. I wait for a few seconds before I knock again as there was no answer. I knock harder because I can hear a television on in the room but still no answer.

She's not here anymore and not answering my calls. I look stupid in this hallway knocking on a hotel room door hoping that a woman who was here more than three weeks ago is still in this room. I'm halfway down the hallway and I hear a woman's voice.

"Kayne!"

I turn around and look back and I notice that it is Jasmine. I can't believe that she is still here. I turn back around and I head toward her room. As I get closer to her I open my arms to give her a hug but she is looking like she isn't pleased to see me and doesn't reciprocate the smile or the open arm greetings.

"What's wrong Jasmine?"

She doesn't say a word and walks away leaving me at the door. I come in and shut the door behind me and I follow her to the bed. I sit down beside her and grab her hand.

"When you sent the text I didn't receive it. I just saw it today and I was hoping that you would still be here so I decided to come and check. I always get your calls and text but some reason these didn't come through."

I show her my phone so that she could also see that I've tried to reach back out to her. "I see that you have tried to contact me Kayne and I have been purposely ignoring you. I found out some things about you that we need to discuss."

I have no clue about what Jasmine is talking about but I'm interested in finding out. This attitude was not what I was expecting coming from her.

"You know why you didn't receive my text Kayne?" Now how she knew the answer to this would be news to me because I have no clue as to how they got past me.

"Who is Olivia?"

At that moment you could hear my face begin to crack into one thousand pieces. "Do you remember when we had a conversation about what was going on in our lives and I never really gave you an answer? Well Olivia is that answer that I wasn't ready to give you that information at the time you asked me because of the fear of the possibility of you passing on me. I knew you had a feeling I was involved with someone but I just wasn't ready to tell you Jasmine."

I can't believe I'm actually admitting a truth to her without even hesitating. It's her eyes that are drawing me in. It's her energy that makes me feel I need to be honest with her because that's the energy she gives me.

It's the feeling of appreciation that I receive from her that she is truly into me and that makes me feel something that I don't feel with Olivia which makes Jasmine a dangerous for me as well as a problem for Olivia.

But how in the hell does she know about her? Jasmine opens the blinds to the room and goes and sits down.

"She came to my room Kayne. She saw the text on your phone. She came here to my fucking room and told me that you and her are together. Living together and how much the both of you are so in love and your plans to marry her."

Ok, the hits just keep on coming my way. How in the hell did Olivia see my text? How did she get into my phone that I always keep locked? I look at my phone again and go back to the text to see the date and time. As I'm scrolling and trying to pin point my lack of discretion. I see the day and the time and I'm thinking…..I'm thinking….and wow, I see where I let my guard down.

Obviously I didn't have my auto lock on my phone because that's the only way she could have gotten in and I was in the shower during the time these text came thru from Jasmine. Fuckkkkkkkkkkkkk!!!!!!!! Oh Olivia is slick. I mean real slick and she played it off so well.

I don't know if I should confront her about this because if I do she will know that I have met up with Jasmine and if I want to keep peace I may have to just keep my mouth shut.

"I don't know what to say Jasmine. I'm sorry that she had the nerve to come here unannounced and approach you. I truly am sorry that she did this."

Jasmine sits calm and remains poised and responds. "She was threatened by me Kayne. A woman knows when there's a threat and she was interested in finding out who could possibly be taking the attention from her so there's no need to apologize for how far a woman will go to get answers."

I'm curious to know more about their interaction so I sit and wait to see if anymore will be revealed.

"The most interesting thing is that she actually thought she was going to come here and persuade me to leave you alone with that information about you and her and hoped that I would be worried. Yes, I was surprised and taken aback a bit but then I said to myself, If Kayne really loved her and was planning on marrying her then he would never try and contact me again. And then you show up today. So you tell me, do I have anything to worry about?" and without hesitation I respond to her.

"No, you don't!"

And just that quick I started the dance in quick sand because when I said that, Jasmine came to me and wrapped her arms around me and gave me a long warm kiss.

"That's all I wanted to hear. I wanted to hear from your mouth that everything that woman said to me doesn't matter and that your interest is wanting to build a future with me. That is what you are saying aren't you?"

Again, my mouth is having its way today as I am no way in control of what its saying.

"That's exactly what I'm saying Jasmine but tell me what is it that you see in me? What is it that you see in me that keeps your interest?" And from the deepest part of her heart she gave me a poetic flow that brought about a feeling that I have only received from the love of my mother.

"When we spent our time together in Jamaica and I heard you speak, it was then I knew I had to have the man that is you. You embody the sensitivity that is required to love me Kayne. It's your voice. Every time you speak to me your voice takes me to places that others words have never taken flight. I know that when I'm with you, I'm with a man. I'm satisfied with you. I'm enamored by you and I have to have you for me. I know we don't have much to go on but I'm interested in finding forever with you. Kayne I would love to find out if forever is us."

Jasmine has just set her flagpole in the ground and claimed her intentions on where she would like home to be and there is no doubt in my mind I am home to her.

I have to admit, her for sureness scares me because I'm really not prepared to get involved with what she desires because I'm in a situation and I refuse to juggle her heart and keep it on string. That just wouldn't be right.

"Jasmine I will not lie to you or play with your feelings. I've had a strong desire to be with you since we've met and I cannot keep the thought of having you off of my mind. There's something about you that gives me an insatiable fixation that I don't want to rid myself of and that intrigues me but I do have this situation that I need to sort through before I can answer the questions of the possibilities of forever with you. When I make my move to allow my emotions to be shifted from its current place I want to do it with ease because when I give it all to you I will want you to know that it is all yours."

She grabs my hands and begins to squeeze them tight. Tears are welling up in her eyes and I know what I have just said to her meant something. "I understand and I appreciate that you care enough about my feelings to do the right thing. I'm leaving to go back home and I won't be back to Los Angeles for a while. There are no pressures from me to make a quick decision because I also want you to know once you have me, I'm all yours Kayne. I just want you to promise me this. If you decide to marry Olivia, just let me know. Will you do that?"

As much as I wanted to give her a promise I knew that I would be lying to her but her gravitational pull and the way she looks at me wouldn't allow my honesty to surface.

"I promise you that Jasmine." And I pull her close to me and give her a hug. I attempted to pull her pants down so that we could make love but she had another way she wanted to end this visit by guiding my hands back around her waist and re-routing my concentration.

"No, I don't want to make love to you again until you are totally mine. Handle what you have too and end what is not good for you. I'll wait for a little while longer. I know that we are supposed to be with other, you just have to accept it."

I couldn't help but to respect her. On one hand she is driving me crazy with her sexual aggressiveness and on the opposite hand she is keeping me at bay with discipline.

"I understand and I respect you Jasmine." She walks me to the door and opens it.

"Don't make me wait too long Kayne. Deep down I know that I love you already, I just can't release it yet."
And she kisses me good bye. I'm walking through the halls of the hotel with many scenarios in my head and decisions to make.

Jasmine just told me her intentions. I want to confront Olivia about her meeting with Jasmine and going through my damn phone. The bullshit with Walter and Regina and her pregnancy news of which I'm hoping has nothing to do with me. My life is in shambles.

As I'm getting in the car my phone begins to ring, I look at the screen and it's my mother.

"Hello Muddah how are you?" Still harboring that bad cough that I noticed on our last conversation, I have to decipher what she is saying closely.

"Hello Kayne. I was just calling you to say I love you. You have been on my mind. I have moved back to Mo Bay because I truly missed home in my older age."

I found that information really surprising because she hadn't spoken to me about making a move back to Jamaica.

"Muddah, when did you move from Florida and why did you do this without telling me?"

All I hear on the other end was her coughing profusely, (COUGH, COUGH, COUGH!). "I didn't want to worry you Kayne. You know me. If I can do it myself, I will, plus Meh Nuh Wan Yuh Tuh Worry Bout Meh."

She knows better than that. I will worry about her regardless. "Do you need anything? Do you need money?" A short pause happens before she replies.

"No, Meh nuh need money No, Yuh come see yah Muddah soon." (COUGH!!! COUGH!!!). I'm a very spiritual person and when I'm moved by Jah's voice it I pay attention.

There was something eerie about my mother's voice and disposition and I knew that she needed me to come and see her soon.

"I'll be there in a few days. You just take care of that cough until I get there."

She laughs at my response.

"You make sure you bring dat gyrl of yours so that I cud meet her finally."

Wow, she wants to meet Olivia. I definitely wasn't expecting this request and I I'm sure Olivia will love it too but I'm not sure if I want to bring her to my sacred place where my soul heals. My mother wants to meet my love and I never want to disappoint her and despite some unresolved shit that I still need to talk with Olivia about I'll wait until after the trip assuming she wants to go.

"Yes Muddah, I will bring her with me. I love you. I love you very much."

"I know son, Yah Muddah loves you more than life. You're the reason why I've lived this long." After I heard this come from my mother's mouth my body was overcome with a very cold feeling like there was meaning to her words. I knew something was wrong and I needed to see my momma. We said our goodbyes and I headed home with my mind racing and my heart heavy.

CHAPTER 16

THE THREAT

Back At Home With Olivia

I come across the card that Walter gave me at the Gala and I'm tempted to call him. That night has been on my mind and I can't seem to shake our conversation. He knows my past too well and I have to make sure that what he knows cannot be revealed.

I have to talk to him to see where his mind is but I know there will be some type of price to pay if I get myself entangled into that web again. I love Kayne too much to have our future ruined by my mistakes in the past and I know how far those brothers will go to ruin a life.

I've seen them put in work and I've seen many lives destroyed as I have helped them destroy many. I can't have him do the same to me so I 'm going to make this call to hopefully come to an understanding with Walter.

I have a new cell phone with a blocked number so I feel comfortable calling without having the risk of him getting my number.

I start dialing the number from the card and it begins to ring. After the third ring Walter answers the phone. "Hello, this is Walter." My heart is beating faster than ever has because I know I shouldn't be making this call but I know that if I don't it will cost me later.

"Hello Walter."

He recognizes my voice immediately and didn't hesitate to be his usual self.

"Well I be damned if it isn't Olivia. I was expecting you to call me and I'm glad that you did. We have to talk my dear and I think you know why, don't you?"

I know what he means and this is why I called. Until I can meet this head on he will forever hang my past over me.

"Walter we need to talk. We need to discuss some things that concern me."

There was a pause over the phone like he was thinking of something real slick to say. "You want to talk to me. You have things that concern you? What concerns do you have? Are you worried that your whoreish past will be found out by your gigolo boyfriend?"

I wasn't prepared to hear this response because I was unaware that he even knew Kayne. This is bad. This is really bad and you could see my heart beating outside of my chest as I know that this meeting will have to take place soon. I have to know what he knows but I now have concerns on meeting him now. Walter can be very nasty when he knows he holds all the cards and if you don't comply he can make your life a living hell.

"Why are you so quiet now Olivia? You didn't think I was going to find out about what was going on with you and with whom? You know I find out what I need to know as my resources run very deep. Yes, I know about your playboy boyfriend and I know that you are in love with him and Alexander can't stand that shit. So yes, we definitely need to meet."

That's a name I didn't want him to bring up at all. I cannot believe that I allowed myself to become entangled with brothers but I was young and needed the money. Yes it was a very stupid move but I had no other choice.

"When will you be available Walter? Can we meet tonight?"

He gives a slight laughter because he knows he has me in his back pocket. "Yes we can meet. You remember the condo downtown don't you?" I answer yes quickly.

"Well you meet me there in an hour." "Ok, I will but can you not tell Alexander that you're meeting with me." He gives another laugh before he responds, "You don't even have to worry Olivia. I will have you all to myself, believe that."

And then he hangs up the phone. I hope he doesn't think this is going to be a fuck meeting because that is not going to happen. Those days are over and I'm not that young girl anymore.

I look at the clock and notice that it's almost eight o'clock. Kayne hasn't made it home yet so I decided that if I leave here now I could possibly be back before he got home. I threw on some sweats and a t-shirt and headed downstairs to my rental not knowing how this meeting is going to turn out but eager to speak my peace and get it over with.

I arrive at Walters's private condo that he has had since I've met him. I go to the security desk and sign in and the guard calls up to tell Walter that I had arrived.

"Congressman, you have a guest here in the lobby. I could hear his voice on the other end of the phone. "Send her up." I head to the elevator and the butterflies in my stomach are going crazy. I'm very nervous about this meeting because I know that the rehashing of my past will be painful as well as finding out what he knows about me and Kayne.

I get to the door and I hesitate before I knock. I take a deep breath and do my best to gather myself. As I go to knock, the door opens and Walter is there standing looking at me. Walter stood 6'5 and weighed more than 275 pounds, He was a large man in stature and his attitude matched.

"Glad you made it, come in Olivia." He grabs my hand and pulls me in the room and closes the door. I go over to the closest seat to the door and sit down. "You look nervous. There's no need to be nervous. We go way back Olivia. You were pregnant with my child."

As he lights a cigar and blows smoke into the circulating fan. He pulls up a chair and sits beside me. "So tell me, what do I owe the honor of your fine ass being here in this familiar place? We must have fucked in every corner, do you remember that? Do you remember when I had about 15 of my constituents in town for the Democratic Convention and you made everybody feel at home for a week? All by yourself too, you must have fucked and sucked until you became numb that week. Don't you remember those good ole days? Damn the memories."

Walter was taking shots at me and he knew it but I'm not going to show him that his words are hurting me.

"Walter, those days are long over. What I want to know is why are you still holding on to the past? Why won't you let that stuff just die?"

He takes a deep inhale from his Cuban and blows smoke directly in my face. "Bitch you don't ask me questions. You don't have the right to ask me shit and when I'm ready to let shit go, I'll let it go when I'm good and damn ready. But let's talk about your boyfriend. Kayne, that's his name right?"

He jumped right in and didn't hesitate to cut to the chase.

"Yes, he is my man and I love him very much and this is why I need to talk to you. Walter I understand that we have a past and I did some things in my past that I should be ashamed of and some of those things I want to remain a secret. This is why I left Alexander. I have a chance at something real and I cannot mess this up. When I saw you at the gala it made me realize that this meeting had to happen."

Walter just looks at me while dropping his ashes in the ashtray. "So you're not going to ask how I know about Kayne."

Of course I want to know but I'm attempting not to seem so eager so I ease into my answer.

"If you would like to tell me, yes I would like to know." Walter gets up from the chair and heads to the bedroom.

"Come with me Olivia." I do not want to leave this living room where I feel that I'm safe but I know Walter so I just get up and follow him to the back because I don't want any problems. When I walk into the room he closes the door and locks it.

"A while back I came across a list that my wife had hidden a while ago and it had some names on it. I didn't make too much of a fuss about it at first until I saw some emails she was sending to this one name that kept showing up all over the place.

But I remained cool and waited to see where it would go. Then she got really bold and started going out and meeting this guy on this list. My wife has been paying good money, my money, to fuck this gigolo and that was the straw that just broken the camel's back and I just found out that she is pregnant by that same guy on that list."

I can't believe what I'm hearing right now. This is not what I was expecting this conversation to be and I'm not ready to hear whose name is on that list that Walter is speaking of but deep down inside I already have a good idea.

I just don't want to hear it and before he reveals the name I plead with him my case because I know what he is about to tell me is not going to be good for anybody involved in this fuckery.

"Walter, I Love….." and he quickly stops me from finishing my sentence.

"Shut the fuck up Olivia!!!!! You are going to hear what I've got to say!" I quickly shut my mouth because he, just like Alexander, has shown me before that he will not hesitate to put hands on a woman.

Walter begins to undress while staring at me still talking.

"Yes, my wife is pregnant from the motherfucker that you are in love with. I've caught my wife on numerous occasions sneaking out to meet Kayne and spending my hard earned money on dick. You know I hired him to do some work for me. Did he tell you that?"

I shake my head No as all of this was a surprise.

"Yes, I had to get close to him. I had to make sure it was the same guy I saw fucking my wife in the middle of the day in a gotdamn parking lots! Is this who you are in love with?!!!" as he begins to walk toward me with bad intentions in his eyes.

"What do you think you are about to do Walter? I didn't come here for this!"

He gets right up on me. This is a mountain of a man and it would be foolish of me to fight him but I can't do what I think he wants me to do so I turn to try and run out of the room but he quickly grabs me and pushes me on the bed. He looks across the room and stares at the closet which seemed very odd to me but that didn't stop him from carrying on

"So what are your plans with Kayne? You plan to marry him Olivia?" as he continues to lay my body down on the bed and straddles me. I'm getting scared now because the look in his eyes doesn't seem like his intentions are going to be friendly.

"Yes, we are going to get married. Walter, please don't do this. Please don't do this to me. I'm not that person anymore."

He is disregarding what I'm saying as he begins to start to pull down my sweats. "Do you want Kayne to know about your past Olivia? Do you want him to know how much of a whore you were? Do you want him to know that the baby you were pregnant with you stuck a hanger up your pussy and killed the baby yourself right here in this room. He doesn't know that you are a murderer does he? And speaking of murder, does Kayne know how many times you helped Alexander hide some of those bodies after the Johns wouldn't pay up after pimping your ass on the streets and he had to make them disappear? Do you want him to know that at one time you were fucking me and my brother at the same time? Or do you want him to know that your father use to fuck you on a regular basis?"

I tried to be strong and not allow his words to get to me but when he brought up my baby and my father I couldn't hold back the tears. He didn't have to force me to do anything. Without a fight I got undressed and conceded to what he was about to do to me. I knew that if I fought it that all of my dirty secrets would be revealed to

Kayne and I couldn't risk that so if fucking Walter will keep his mouth shut then that's the price I'm going to have to pay for his silence.

"So if you want me to keep my mouth closed you are going to open your filthy legs and you are going to fuck me until I'm tired do you understand me?" As he now is completely on top of my naked body with my legs spread open.

"Walter can you please use a condom? I don't want to have sex without one." He just looks at me and ignores my request and proceeds to enter my body. Tears still streaming from the sides of my eyes, I just turn my head to the side and took what he had to give me and for an hour. I just laid there like a worthless piece of flesh.

When it was all said and done I got up and started to put on my clothes. I say to him, "So are we even now? Are you going to keep my past in the past and let me be fucking happy Walter?"

He begins to laugh at me like I had told the funniest joke. "You want all of this to be in the past Olivia?

You want me to forget all the great things we accomplished so that you can go and run off and marry that two bit dick for hire boyfriend?"

"Yes, I want you to leave me the fuck alone and let me be happy. I want you and Alexander to leave me the fuck alone!!!"

Walter gets his naked and sweaty body up and heads toward the direction that he was staring at and opens a sliding panel and pulls out a camera.

"These cameras these days are really efficient. They don't use tapes anymore. They use Bluetooth and Wi-Fi. Yes, everything that is recorded automatically is saved to a hard drive in the computers that is synched. Technology sure has advanced since our earlier days fucking on camera. Do you remember how much we use to do that Olivia?"

This is unbelievable. This motherfucker has taped this whole thing.

"I can't believe you did this Walter. You are a shady bastard. I should have known better than to come here and reason with you."

Shaking his head at what I just said. "You are still the dumbest bitch on the planet. Olivia I will always stay ahead of the gotdamn game. Yes, you should have known better. Now listen to me. Kayne doesn't have to know anything about your past or about tonight but you have to agree to something now. This is very critical are you listening?" I nod my head yes and continue to listen.

"For reasons that I cannot wrap my head around, my brother is still in love with you and I promise you he will not stop until he gets you back."

I don't know where Walter is going with this but he's mentioning Alexander's name for a reason.

"You can't marry Kayne. That shit will never happen Olivia and if you think you can get away with it, just try me. You fucking try me. I promise you that I will tell Kayne everything and he will see this video. Alexander won't be too happy either because I'll tell him that you needed money and you came to me instead of him and promised me the best night of my life if I gave it to you. He's my brother but he doesn't know our deep history and you know how angry he can get don't you? So it looks like you have to make a very hard decision my dear. I sure wouldn't want to be you right now."

The threat was made and I heard it loud and clear. The only thing I could do was pick my feelings and face off the floor and leave. "Take care Olivia and thank you for everything. Oh, and I'm sorry about the truck. I tried to stop Alexander but you know how much of a hard head his ass can be. Well at least I stopped him from shooting Kayne that night."

I shut the door in disgust as I couldn't believe what had just happened and the information that I found out about Kayne. As I'm driving back home I begin to just bawl. My life could have been so different if my childhood wasn't so fucked up and I had the make choices then that I'm paying for today.

Now I'm faced with the possibility of not marrying the man who truly has my heart because of my secrets. If Kayne knew my truth there's no way in hell he would want to marry me. We both have a past but even with the skeletons we both share there's a limit that anyone can take and I know for a fact my skeletons may be too much to accept.

My drive home was the longest ride I've ever had and I was praying that I made it back before Kayne so that I could hurry and clean my body from the filth of Walter. I really want to confront Kayne about his dealings with Walters's wife and I damn sure want to know if he knows that she is pregnant and why he didn't tell me that he was hired to do some work for Walter.

That is why he asked to see him at the gala. It's all making sense now and Walter was with Alexander that night our vehicles were destroyed.

I knew eventually I would have to deal with my past and it has come back to bite me in my ass. I drive in and park. I see that Kayne hasn't made it home yet. I rush upstairs and I turn on the shower.

I go and take the clothes that I had on and put them in a plastic bag and put it in the garbage chute. I wanted to do my best to erase the night from my mind and everything else that was attached to it.

As the hot water began to steam up the bathroom I just sit and let the streams of water wash my reality away.

After 20 minutes of me crying and trying to remove the truth from my mind I hear Kayne come thru the door and calls my name.

"Olivia, I'm home." I turned off the water and get out of the shower to dry off. Kayne comes to the bathroom and opens the door.

"Baby, you want to go to Jamaica?" After the night I just had, I needed to get away and clear my head.

"Yes, how soon can we leave?" "We will leave this week. My mom has moved back home and I need to go and see her. Something isn't right and she is not sounding good. She wanted me to bring you to meet you."

I'm very surprised to hear this. Kayne has been very secretive about our relationship to his mother and I was shocked to hear that she wanted to meet me.

"She really wants to meet me? This is big Kayne." "Yes it is babe. She wants to meet the woman I'm in love with and going to marry one day soon. Start packing. We will be there for about a week or so."

And he closes the door and heads out to the room. She wants to meet the woman he is about to marry? This is not what I needed to hear. Fuck me.

CHAPTER 17
WINGS

The sun was shining bright once we landed at Sangster International Airport. Olivia was in awe of what she was laying her eyes upon. She had never been out of California much less the country and Montego Bay was the paradise that awakened her spirit and she saw first-hand why I become alive when I come home.

"Wow, Kayne this is such a beautiful place; it looks like a post card."

I loved to see her excitement about my birthplace and I couldn't wait to show her around but that would have to wait.

I needed to get to the countryside so that I could see my mother. After we gathered our bags we headed to pick up our rental car and headed toward the country. The curving roads provided a picturesque scene as we drove along the cliffs that were surrounded by mountains. The air was clean and the summer's heat provided the glistening balm that covered our bodies as we rode with the top down.

I look over to Olivia and I see that she has already fallen in love with the mystique of Jamaica. She turns to me and blows me a kiss while we both took in the sounds of Bob Marley's *Could You Be Loved played* in the background.

My family still had a small piece of property in Maroon town in the Saint James Parish and that's where my mother was. It was her birthplace where her and her siblings were raised and every year she would return from Florida to get a taste of home.

She really never wanted to leave Jamaica but did so after she had gotten remarried when my father passed away.

Florida never felt like her comfort zone because she was always coming back to here. Once her second husband died she decided to stay in Florida and take care of the belongings they had accumulated over the years but her heart remained in Ja. The news that she would be returning bothered me and this is why I can't wait to lay my eyes on my queen. I have some questions to ask her.

I pull up to the home, park the car and I look to Olivia.

"Well we are here. You are about to meet my mother. Are you ready?"

You can tell that she was very nervous but she managed to give me a smile and respond, "I think so." I give her a kiss and we get out of the car and head to the house. The screen door is open and I yell into the home. "

Marie JoAnn…!!!" Anytime I called my mom by her name she would laugh and always reply, "Yuh don't Call mi muh name bwoi, Meh Muddah to yah!" and we would laugh and hug each other but there was no response this time.

An eerie feeling has come over me and Olivia has taken notice. I notice that my mom is not in the living room so I ask Olivia to just sit tight for a minute so that I can go and see where mom is. I call out again, "Muddah, where are you?"

Still no answer. So I head to the back room and slowly open the door and there I see that mother is asleep in bed. It has been a while since I've seen her and I could tell immediately something was wrong. She didn't look like she was full of energy and her radiant vibes wasn't visible anymore.

She appeared worn down and her head was full of grey hair. Mother never allowed her grey hair to grow in which was a sign that things were not quite right.

I slowly close the door because I didn't want to wake her and I go back into the living room where Olivia was.

"Is everything ok Kayne? Is your mom here?" Looking around in the home that I spent summers in as pictures of my family adorned the walls I responded, "Yes, she is the back room and asleep. I didn't want to wake up. Let's put our things away and I'm going to get in the kitchen and cook dinner so when she wakes up food will be ready."

I show Olivia where our room would be and she heads there to unpack and to wash her travels clean with a shower.

I go into the kitchen to see what my mom has to cook and I notice that she has already shopped and has *evahting* that I considered my favorite. Cooking was something that I always loved to do and to cook authentic Caribbean food was my specialty.

I've prepared many meals for Olivia before but I've never cooked a full blown Jamaican meal for her and I can't wait. I immediately get to work in my preparation and it didn't take long before I had the entire house smelling like spices.

Olivia must have taken a nap as well because by the time she wakes I was turning down the heat on the brown stew Jamaican chicken and onions, a side dish of cabbage and carrots sautéed with vinegar , spices and hot Chile pepper, rice and peas and a loaf of coconut bread that mother already had.

The aromas awakened everyone in the house because before you knew it Olivia had made her way into the kitchen. "Kayne, I don't know what you have cooked but it smells good" as she goes over and looks in the pots. From the back room we hear my mother.

"Who dey hav dem pots pon mi stove tahhking?" The sweetest voice in the room has awaken and I turn to see my muddah standing with her arms opened wide smiling at me.

I dropped everything and like a little boy I run to her and give her a big hug and a kiss. Her hugs were the comfort that brought me back to my childhood and my soul said hello to hers and we reconnected for about five minutes, mother to son as tears flowed from our eyes.

Olivia just stood and watched us have our moment while her eyes began to fill with water as well.

When mother notices Olivia stand there in the kitchen, she removes her thick accent and says, "Who may this be Kayne. Is this the princess that you spoke to me about?"

She walks over to Olivia with open arms and gives her a hug. "Hello ma'am, I am Olivia, nice to meet you." Mother looks at me and gives me a wink, "You're a pretty girl, nice to meet you too baby and welcome to Jamaica. Please excuse this old lady and all of this grey hair but chile I don't give a shit at this point."

Olivia will learn fast that my mother has a very good sense of humor as she brought us all to laughter. It is good to see my mom smiling although she still appeared to be weak and frail. "You are still beautiful, grey or not." Mom looks at me again, "Yah bettah keep dis one heah son; she know truth when it's in her eyes."

This couldn't have turned into a better introduction. I sit my mother down at the table and Olivia and I began to prepare to eat our first meal together in my homeland of Jamaica. We are all having a good time laughing, listening to mom tell old childhood stories about her life and about us growing up.

Olivia is taking it all in and hanging on to every word that she is saying. "Ms. Marie, can you tell me how Kayne was as a child?" She smiles and begins to cough.

"Excuse me, but Kayne was a sweet boy. He never gave me problems at all. He was attentive and always made sure that I was ok. He was my overseer and was nosey when it came to my business." She laughs, (COUGH, COUGH!!) and resumes with laughter.

Hearing that cough and watching her struggle through it really bothered me so I had to inquire about it before she told another childhood story.

"Mom, what is that cough that you have? I noticed that on our last conversation and I see that it's worse than I imagined it to be." She throws her hand up at me as if to say, no worries. "Don't you worry about me son, your mother is fine. It's just an old person's cough. This happens when you get old. Your body starts to do things that you don't have answers too."

That sounded all cute and everything but I wasn't buying it. "Have you gone to see the doctor for it?" She notices that I'm not smiling and is very serious about this question. "No I haven't son, I've been afraid to go."

I'm sitting here looking at this frail woman who I have never known to be afraid of anything saying this to me and I can't believe it. "Mom, you can't be serious. You have money and insurance that I make sure that you keep so there's no excuse for you not to be going to check on your health. First thing in the morning, I will be taking you to town to see the doctor about that cough ok?"

Mom looks at Olivia, "See what I mean, he will always take care of me and that's why he will always be my first born baby."

She kisses me on the forehead. And we continue to finish our dinner.

"Son dinner was good as well as the conversation but yah Muddah is tired. I'm gwan take a bath and head to bed. We got an early morning to tend too."

I help her stand from the table and give her a hug. "See you tomorrow Ms. Marie, sleep well."

Mother looks back at Olivia and smiles and heads to the back room. "You're worried about her aren't you baby?" I'm definitely not concealing my concern too well and Olivia knows it. "Olivia, something isn't right. This is not my mom's usual self and she is not telling me the truth."

She comes over and gives me a hug and looks into my eyes. "Everything will be alright Kayne. Your mother will be fine. Ask all of the questions tomorrow when you take her to the doctor."

She is right, I'm worried but I will just have to wait to find out more answers about my mom's health so in the meantime I'm going to clean the kitchen up and take Olivia on a country walk while my mother gets her rest.

Again, being here makes me forget about all of the drama that I left back in Los Angeles. There is a safety that Jamaica gives me and deep down inside I miss being here full time. In a perfect world this would be home for me to be shared with the love of my life but as my complicated life would have it that will be a fairy-tale which will remain to be seen.

The kitchen is cleaned up and we have dressed in our walk attire headed out to enjoy the sounds and sights of my country.

"I can't believe how beautiful this place is Kayne and you grew up here?" We are surrounded by the mountains and streams. The serenity the countryside gives you makes you forget the concrete jungles of the city. I could see the worries that Olivia may have had are being replaced with wide eye gazing and pointing at the sights. It's been over an hour now and the sun has begun to set behind us and it's time for us to return home for the evening.

"Kayne, can we stop for a minute. I would like to talk with you before we get back to the house."

There's a wooden bench located off the side of the dirt road where we're walking so I grab her hand and lead her there to sit and talk.

"What's up baby?" "I knew this is a big deal for you to bring me with you to meet your mother and I'm so appreciative of it. I want you to know that I don't take this meeting lightly. I know it means more to you than just a 'meeting'. You are introducing me to the woman you love the most in your life."

I don't know where Olivia is going with this but I remain engaged.

"Lately we have been living with the elephant in the room and neither one of us has really addressed the many issues that we know we have. Let me be the first to say; I'm sorry if I've caused you pain because that's not my intension. I don't mean to. There are things in my spirit that have not healed. Sometimes I don't know how to articulate my feelings in a way that helps you understand me. So often many times things may go unconfirmed which causes friction between us; I know that has to stop if we are going to be together."

I don't know what has gotten into Olivia right now but she is surprising me with her truth moment.

Personally, I have stuff going on too and I can relate to what she is saying and I whole-heartedly agree. These lies and going behind each other's back has to stop if we would like to continue our life together. A part of me wants to lay everything out on the table and be free from the secrets that are binding me but if I make that choice it may cause more problems than we already have. Is this her moment where she just wants to come clean with me? Is she going to reveal her secrets that I somewhat know about but still needs confirmation? Is there more to her story that I'm clueless about? Sometimes, being here on the countryside relaxes your spirit so much that you find yourself opening up. There is an energy that can only be emitted and received here; no place can offer you that feeling which makes me crave being back on the island.

Jasmine flashes across my mind as I listen to Olivia give me her heart felt truths.

I keep hearing Jasmine's voice say, "*Come home…Come home,*" and as I look into Olivia's eyes, her words have become muted because of the mirage of Jasmine's face has taken over.

"Kayne, are you listening to me? I asked you a question." Do you think you could see us living here forever?"

I totally didn't hear shit after the image I was having of Jasmine. How ironic that she would be asking me that question right now.

"Jamaica is a beautiful place anyone could call home Liv." The look on her face tells me that wasn't answer she was expecting. "Yes baby, I agree but I'm talking about you and I Kayne."

I pretend that I was joking and I grab her around the waist and kiss her, "Of course my love." She playfully hits me on the shoulder and laughs.

"Actually Liv, I feel the same way that you feel and I would also like to apologize for all of my wrong doings too. I just want us to be happy baby. I understand we both have some past issues and we both are struggling with our demons. In order for us to release them, we have to be completely honest with other."

Now I know what I was saying was partly true. I wasn't prepared at all to tell Olivia what I knew but I wanted to see if she was.

"Is there anything else that I need to know Olivia? Are there anymore secrets?"

The sun is just below the horizon and the night creatures are beginning to make music around us. There is a cool breeze that is coming off the Caribbean Sea that is not far from my mother's house. The scene could have easily been written in a movie. Olivia grabs my hands and stands up. She looked into my eyes and says, "I will never hold another secret from you Kayne. Tonight will mark the night that forever actually stands a chance with us."

And she gives me a long kiss. My heart wanted to believe Olivia but my mind knew the truth as she was clearly lying to me. Yes, I'm sure she meant what she said. She doesn't know that I a few things but for the sake of not making this a pleasant trip; I'm not going to say anything different at this moment. She is in her truth. Who am I to tell her that her truth is a motherfucking lie waiting to let out of the closet? Not me, as we share some of the same skeletons and the bones are vying position.

"What about you Kayne? Is there anything that you have to tell me? Is there anything that you have to say? I want this to be the moment where we can let everything out because when we leave to go back home we will bury the drama in the sands of Montego Bay never to be recovered again."

My heart agrees with her but my mind is fights it tooth and nail. From the look in Olivia's eyes, she desperately believes what she is saying. Maybe I can just throw caution to the wind and forget what waits for the both of us in California. Hell, we don't even have to go back and truly make it a reality. There will be no more Alexander, Walter, on the clock appointments and no more bullshit. I grab her hand and kiss it softly.

"Baby there aren't any more secrets. Let's just live, be happy and see where the future takes us." She jumps up, wraps her legs around my waist and kisses me. I guess that was music to her ears. Everything is settled for now and I'm cool with that.

We continue our trek back home as we watch the sun disappear beneath the horizon. We reach home and the house is completely dark; mom has already settled in from the evening. I go to her room and I peek inside and see that she is fast asleep. I walk over to the bed, bend over and kiss her forehead goodnight.

Morning Comes Early and Kayne is Still Asleep

I'm up before everyone so I begin to prepare breakfast. It's not long before Ms. Marie wakes and heads to the kitchen to do the same but finds that she has been beaten to the punch.

"Good morning Ms. Marie, I hope that you don't mind that I prepare breakfast for everyone." (COUGH! COUGH!). She sits down and smiles at me.

I could tell that she wasn't feeling well but tried to have a conversation anyway. "No baby, that is fine. You make yourself right at home." I fix her plate and place it in front of her. "Would you like some juice?" Mom shakes her head yes while taking a small bite of her toast. "So are you ready to go to the doctor to see about your cough Ms. Marie?"

She doesn't answer me right off but continues to eat her breakfast. I don't want to impose so I don't ask her again. I sit down and begin to eat my breakfast. It's not long before I can see tears streaming from Ms. Maries eyes."

When I see this, I immediately get up and go to her. "Is everything ok?" She just puts her head in her hands and begins to bawl. I don't know what to do because I don't want to overstep boundaries. "Do you want me to go and wake up Kayne Ms. Marie?" She shakes her head no and continues to cry.

"You know my health isn't good Olivia and it hasn't been for a while. I lied to my son yesterday when I told him that I was afraid to go the doctor. Truth is, I've been going but I just didn't want to tell him what was wrong with me because I know he won't take the news too. I know he'd leave California to come and take care of me."

I sit at the table confused at what Kayne's mother is saying but scared to hear more because I know that the information she has kept from her son is important.

"Ms. Marie, I don't mean to pry into your business and please do tell me if I'm over stepping my boundaries but what is wrong? What is it that you don't want to tell Kayne?"

Ms. Marie looks around to make sure that Kayne is nowhere to be seen and motions to me to go outside and sit on the porch with her. We leave the kitchen and head outside and sit in the chairs on the porch.

"Olivia, I'm very sick and I didn't want to tell Kayne because he has his own life in Los Angeles. I just didn't want to worry my son with my stuff."

My eyes start to tear up because I know this is serious and she is entrusting me with some vital information.

"Ms. Marie, I don't know what's wrong but you have to tell Kayne. He loves you more than life itself and you know that; he will do everything in his power to help you. He loves you to death so please tell him. Are you afraid that he will find out what's wrong with you today when he takes you to the doctor?"

Those words must have hit something in her heart because she broke down into pieces, all I could do was hold her in my arms and rock with her until she calmed down. While she's resting her head on my chest, she looks up and says to me, "I want you to take care of my son. He's a good man and has been through a lot. Love him and stand behind him. He has been disappointed a lot in his life and he doesn't need any more disappointments ok?" I nod, yes. "Now I need you to promise me that. Promise you will not hurt my son."

……..Olivia reckons with herself, I have no intentions on hurting Kayne, ever, and despite my darkest secrets that will keep me from being 100% honest, I will do my best to keep my promise to his mother………..

"I promise Ms. Marie, I will never hurt Kayne." She gives me a long hard stare and I could feel her spirit testing my soul because warmth overcame me and it seems like we both believe that everything was going to be ok…for now.

Kayne Wakes Up

We head back into the house and go back to the kitchen to finish our breakfast. We both see that Kayne has awakened and is fixing his plate. He turns and sees us walking in.

"Well good morning ladies, where have y'all been?" I begin pouring a glass of juice as Ms. Marie sits down to finish eating her breakfast.

"Son, we just had some girlfriend talk that's all. You know I had to ask some questions." She laughs but it's soon followed by a succession of coughs. (COUGH! COUGH! COUGH………..)

"Well as soon as we are done eating we are going to go to the doctors to see about that cough ok?" Mom looks up at me and smiles before she gives a sarcastic remark, "Yes daddy, I hear you!" We all laugh at her comment and finish our breakfast together.

"I'm going to stay here while you take your mom to the doctor Kayne. I have to clean the kitchen anyways. Go and be with your mother, I'll be fine until you get back."

Mom gets up and walks back to her room to get dressed and leaves me and Olivia in the kitchen. "How was she this morning? What did she say to you?"

"Oh nothing baby. Like your mother said we just had some girl talk about love and life but I will tell you this, she loves her son more than anything in the world."

And she gives me a quick kiss and goes back to cleaning the kitchen. I smile because it's moments like this that make me happy. Both of my ladies are getting along, I'm home in Jamaica and my spirit is opening up to what could possibly be.

Mom and I head into town to visit our family doctor who I haven't seen me in years. He never fails to give my mother the best medical care. We walk into the office and we are cheerfully greeted by the receptionist.

She gives us the necessary papers to fill out and tells us to wait in the lobby area; she will call us when it's time to go in the back.

After about a 20 minute wait, Dr. Cornelius comes from the back to greet us. "Ah Marie, glad to see yuh mi darling. Wen yuh come back pon de bay? "And he reaches down to give her a hug.

"Kayne!!!!! Mi nuh seen yuh since you was a teenager. How yuh been young bruddah?" "I've been doing well Dr. Cornelius. Still working and living in Los Angeles."

You can see how happy he was to see me and my mother. He was around my mother's age and I could have sworn at one time he had a crush on her but never acted upon it because my mother was married. Nonetheless, they remained good friends and he always made sure when she was home he would take care of her.

As he is looking over the paperwork I can tell he is making mental notes before he ask questions. "Marie, tell me about yah cough. How long it's been?" Mom looks at me before she answers the question like she really doesn't want me to hear the answer but answers him anyways.

"Cornelius, I've had this cough for a few years now."

I'm now looking at my mother in disbelief because she has never told me about this and for this to be a problem that has existed for so long, it's just not good.

"Ok, let's go to the back and let me take a look and run some test Marie." He grabs her hand and walks her to the back room. I get up to go with them but my mother turns back and says to me, "No son, you stay here. You know that I'm private about my business and there's no need for you to come. If there's anything serious I'll be sure to tell you."

I do not like that at all but I have to respect her wishes. I look to doc and say, "Dr. Cornelius please let me know what's going on with my Muddah." He smiles and continues to lead her to the back.

"Yuh gwan sit yuh butt down bwoi, yuh Muddah gwan beh fine." Reluctantly, I go and sit down and I wait and wait and wait.

It's been close to an hour and I'm getting worried that I haven't heard anything so I go to the receptionist and ask if she could go back and see if everything was ok. She agrees and I go back to have a seat until she returned with some answers for me.

I sit for a few more minutes and she comes from the back.

"Dr. Cornelius beh still with yah Muddah, him will be done shortly."

It is now going on two hours and my Muddah comes from the back without Dr. Cornelius.

"What's going on? Where's doc? I have some questions."

"Kayne, he is busy right now. He gave me all the information that I needed and medicine for my cough. He told me to tell you that it was nice seeing you and he will see you next time."

"Well mom, how are you? What test did he run? What did he say? Did he give you a diagnosis?"

Mom grabs my face and pulls me close to her. "I'm fine, you need not worry. Stop asking me so many questions. Let's go, get Olivia and get some lunch" And she walks out of the office. I look back just to see if the Doc would be coming to say bye or to give me any information but he doesn't and I follow mother out of the office frustrated and confused.

While driving home there is an eerie quietness in the car that seems forced. Mom knows I want to know more about her visit and I know she isn't going to offer any information.

"Mom, what did the doctor say? Why are you being so secretive about your health? Is there something serious going on?"

Mom gives me a stern look and responds. "You just won't leave me alone about my health will you? I've told you before I'm going to be fine and if it was anything serious I would let you know. It's not serious. Cornelius gave me some medicine and said that I should be fine in a week or so and the cough would go away. I need for you to stop worrying Kayne."

It's taking everything within me not to fight her on this and usually I would but I know she is not in the best of health and my prying and agitating her will most likely make issues worst so I swallowed my interest and we enjoy the rest the ride. We rode in silence and allowed the cool summer breeze to brush across our faces.

A few days have passed now and the visit has gone pretty well. Olivia and my mother have hit it off. They have been spending time together taking walks and going shopping in town leaving me in the distance. I didn't mind though. I wanted Olivia to experience the woman who gave me life as well as my first dose of unconditional love.

My mother is everything to me and I don't know how I would fare if I didn't have her in my life. It's a blessing to have such a love and respect for someone who has given me everything that she had in life and all I want to do as her child is to repay her with everything that she has ever wanted.

As the days continued to go by I was realizing that my time on the islands was about to come to an end. I wasn't necessarily eager to return to Los Angeles because I still had the drama on my mind when I left but it is my home now and I will make the best of it.

Olivia asked me to take her to Dunn's River Falls in Ocho Rios because I told her stories about when I use to go there with friends and family; I promised I'd take her.

I was going to take my mom on the trip too because she used to love sitting and allowing the mist from the waterfalls to splash her while watching the kids jump around and play in the crystal clear blue waters. The night before the trip we sit out on the porch and had a conversation about life in general and how roadblocks would come about to keep us all from happiness.

It was like school was in session when my mother spoke. She had so much knowledge and was willing to share it with anyone who was eager to listen.

"Kayne, I want you to know that I'm so proud of you with all that you have accomplished. I'm also glad that you have found someone who has brought you peace and I hope that you are just as happy with my son Olivia."

Olivia is hanging on to my mom's every word while holding her hand.

"Love is a very special word but it takes actions to give that word life. Love doesn't hurt nor disappoint. If you ever allow it to do those two things then you will discover that Love doesn't really exist; you are forcing the Love to do things it's not capable of doing. Love requires sacrifice and support; it's forever a fulltime commitment for the two people to build a life together. Love is the anchor; it is the force that will hold of you steady. If you do not pay attention to that anchor, your ships will drift away, never to cross paths again."

As I'm listening to my mother drop these words of wisdom in our ears, I see tears collecting in her eyes but she remains fluid in her conversation.

"Mom, do you miss being married?" She takes a long pause, a deep breath before answering. "Son, I loved being married. When your father was alive, he was my best friend and we did everything together. He was a Real man. He provided for his family and was strong in his beliefs. I never challenged him because I knew he would never put us in harm's way. You remind me a lot of your father because you are stubborn just like he was. He was a fixer and he loved hard. You could always count on him. That's what I miss about being married. When I remarried after your father died, it just wasn't the same. Only one anchor mattered and the other ship sailed away from me."

By this time we are all in tears because you can feel the pain in her words and the loneliness in her heart. Holding Olivia's hand, she stares into her eyes and asks her a question.

"Do you love my son? Olivia kisses my mother's hand and responds. "Ms. Marie I have never loved anyone else as much as I love Kayne.

My mother then turns to me and asks the same question. "Son, do you love Olivia, like I think you do?"

My passions and convictions are pricked and before I knew it, without a second thought or any premeditation, I say, "Mother, I have loved Olivia from the moment I laid eyes on her. She has awakened my heart from a dormant sleep. I didn't think I could find the type of woman who could bring the emotions that I feel for her to the surface but she has made me feel things that I know only Love would allow. Yes, it has not always been this way, we have had our moments of clouded clarity but my love for her finds a way to remain attached to the forever that is waiting for us."

Olivia is drowning in tears at this point because she hears me express my love for her to the Queen. I had become caught up in the moment too and my own tears were gathering into a puddle on the old wooden boards.

"Son, when a man finds a wife he has found a good thing."

Nothing else needed to be said; we both received the message. I looked at Olivia and she looked at me. I pulled her close and kissed her like I had never kissed her before as the lighting bugs provide an orange tinted fireworks display. It was getting late. We had to go to bed and get rest for our big day in Ochos.

"Mom are you excited about going to the falls again? She flashes me with that big West Indian yardie gyal smile and says, "Meh Bwan ready son, meh cannot wait" and gives me a high five.

"Well my children let me go in here and darken these grey hairs before tomorrow. You know yah Muddah have to look cute before she goes somewhere. I may find me a new husband!"

Her humor never ceases to amaze me and Olivia again has experienced her wit. She gives us both a kiss but while giving me mine she whispers in my ear, "You better marry this woman," And walks toward her room for the rest of the night.

There was something she must have felt tonight and she co-signed her belief in Olivia that she was fit for me. They say mothers always know best especially when it comes to their sons.

I've been fighting my love for Olivia because I've been selfish in ways that would only benefit me and my mother knew this about her son. There was a reason why she said all that she said this past week and tonight; it all came together. Olivia kisses me before she heads in for the night. "Baby, I love you. Don't be too long, we have a long day tomorrow. I'm so excited!!" and she heads to the room. I remain seated rocking back and forth in the old rocking chair and listen to the crickets serenade me until my eyelids got heavy.

Morning came quick but I woke up full of energy and I was ready to hit the road to head to the falls. I look over to Olivia and wake her. "Good morning my love, time to get up." She opens one eye and responds, "Is it morning already?" I reach under the covers and begin to rub her sleepy flower. "Ohhhhhh no Kayne, I will not let you do this to me; we are not going to have sex in your mother's house. I'm in her good graces now!"

As we both laugh and she wiggles herself out of the bed and heads to the shower. I get out of bed and head to the kitchen to cook a quick breakfast for everyone. I have Peter Tosh playing in the background and I'm swaying to the melodic sounds as the rich aroma of turkey bacon fills the room. I yell out to the ladies, "Breakfast is ready, come and eat. It's a beautiful day in Jamaica!!"

Olivia does her best impression of lip synching to the words that I had just spoken but is failing miserably because she is tone deaf and a horrible singer. She puts her arms around my waist and we dance while I'm singing to her.

"Muddah, up and at em!!!!! Let's go let's go!!"

We sit for breakfast as I've fixed everyone's plate. Mom has not come from her room and she didn't respond to my call. Maybe she is still asleep and the smells of this good breakfast didn't wake her up.

"Go and wake her Kayne before her breakfast gets cold." Realizing that Olivia was right, I get up from the table and I head to her bedroom and knock. A few seconds pass and there's no response so I knock harder and wait.

"Mom, are you awake?" Still no answer, so I slowly open her door and peek in and I see that she is still fast asleep in the bed. I push the door open a little wider and walk into the room to wake her so that we could get our day started.

She looked beautiful with her freshly dyed jet black hair. She had on the beautiful long white night gown that made her look like an angel. As I got closer to sit on the bed so that I could gently rub her shoulder to wake her I notice a bright red stain on her sheets.

I go in closer as I shake her shoulder and notice the bright red color can also be seen on her gown.

"Mom...wake up, it's time to eat so we can go to the falls." There is no response and she isn't moving. I put my hand on her face to rub her cheek and notice that her body is cold. I shake her and yell louder, "Momma, wake up...wake up momma!"

By this time, Olivia has heard my voice and has walked to the door. "Is everything ok Kayne?!"

I grab my mother and move her body and notice that the bright red stains that I see on the sheets and on her gown is blood that has leaked from her nose and mouth; she wasn't breathing. Everything was happening in slow motion. I try and lift her from the bed and all I could feel was her cold bodies as the weight of her just covered me like a blanket.

I yell out to Olivia, "Oh my godddddd! She's gone!!!! She's dead Olivia!!!! No, please Jah you can't take her from me!" Olivia runs in and sees my mother's lifeless body in my arms and blood now covers my shirt and just screams. Nooooooooooooooooooooo!!!! Nooooooo!!!!" and covers her mouth at the sight of the man who she loves holding his deceased mother in his arms bawling like a baby.

"Mommy, come back, please come back, don't you leave me!" and I shake her lifeless body. I knew that she was gone but a part of me was wishing that she was just in a deep sleep and could be awakened by my shakes. Jah has spoken, given my mother her wings and took her home.

Olivia was frozen in shock and was crying hysterically because there was nothing that she could do to calm me.

I just held my mom and rocked until my tears covered both of our bodies. I held on to her so tight that the warmth of my body began to warm her once cold flesh. I know that Jah calls his Angels when he sees fit but today I became angry with Him because He didn't consider the hole that would be vacant in my heart from His decision. My understanding quickly turned into anger as I just lay in the bed like a small child spending my last moments with my Queen.

Slow motion is still the energy in the room as I get up and walk past Olivia who is now sitting on the floor with her head down and I go to the living room to call the paramedics. This day marks the ending of a love that could never be replaced.

Olivia comes into the living room and hands me an envelope.

"This was on her bed Kayne."

It was addressed to me and while trying to gather myself by wiping the tears from my face I open the envelope to see what was inside. She had written me a letter before she took her last breath.

"Son, I want you to know I knew this day would be coming soon. Jah and I have had many conversations and I knew that my time on earth was not going to be forever and He needed me with him to spread love. I couldn't bear to look in your eyes and hurt you so I remained silent with what ailed me. I told Cornelius to stay in his office and to wait until we left the office on my appointment day and had him promise me that he wouldn't call you and reveal the truth. He is a man of his word and I knew he would abide by my last wishes. Cancer has had its way with me for the last 10 years and I tried to fight it with all my might. When I visited you at your home I was coming to tell you then but I quickly realized that you needed me more than I needed you and I kept silent and made sure my baby boy was going to be ok. Like your father, I know that you may be heartbroken and angry and I apologize to you but my love for you son, wouldn't allow me to hurt you face to

face. I saw the angels on the porch tonight when we were talking and I knew then it was my time to go. I love you son. I want happiness for you. Remember what I whispered in your ear and I'll be watching you from above. …..Mommy

All of my strength left me at that moment and I just fell to the floor crying. Olivia lay next to me consoling me while trying to rock the pain away. I could hear the blare of the ambulance sirens in the near distance as it got closer to our home.

I remained in the fetal position as the paramedics rushed through the door and Olivia pointed them to the room where my mother's body was. As my heart is beating loudly and my eyes are bloodshot red I see the paramedics are now wheeling my mom out of the house on the gurney.

This is the finale and my last goodbye to my Queen. I motion for them to stop her body in front of me and I pull back the sheets that covered and I kiss her on her forehead.

"Meh gwan always luv yuh Muddah…Jah Bless" and I pull the sheet over her and they wheel her out of the house.

I remember having a conversation with her long ago and she told me whenever she passed away she didn't want a big fuss and to keep it simple as cremation was her choice and she wanted her ashes to be spread into the Caribbean sea.

I would honor my mother's wishes a week later. I contacted my brother and a few family and friends. The news shocked everyone and they didn't hesitate getting to Jamaica to pay their respects.

It was good to see my baby brother as we shared the pain of losing our mother. All of my closest childhood friends showed up as well and told all the stories about their times in our home with mom around.

I could see the pain on my brother's face; it was not easy for him to accept that mother was gone. He promised he would come to visit me more often.

He and Olivia got along too as they talked and shared laughter from the stories he told of him and I growing up as kids. Relatives near and far heard the news and although mother wanted it to be small the church was a packed house as they gave her a celebratory Queens Day send away.

June 24th will always be a day etched into my heart as that was the day that Jah decided to give my mother her wings so that she could forever fly with the other angels who protected their sons. Marie Joann……..I will always love you.

CHAPTER 18

THE DECISION

On Kanye's Mind

It's been close to a month since my mother's death our life has returned to a bit of normalcy. I have not been on the clock, quite frankly, I am not interested in that life. My heart is still hemorrhaging from the loss of my mother and Olivia has been doing an excellent job with helping my cope.

We have been spending a lot of time together in our new place just loving on each other. I haven't had any run-ins with Walter or Alexander and that's good because I really don't have any patience for their shit at this point in my life.

Although I have been receiving emails and text messages from Jasmine checking in on me and sending her condolences after she learned about my mother's death. She apologizes for not being able to attend the services; I respect her for that, besides it bothers me because I didn't expect for her to show up.

Olivia was there and I just didn't need that confusion. A part of me is attempting to distance myself from Jasmine and hopefully she will get the picture because I am being very short with my responses to her.

She said she was giving me time to make a decision about my relationship with Olivia and I respected her for that. The words that my mother spoke to me sank into my heart and soul and in order for me to build something strong I have to be honest and drop my anchor with Olivia.

Yes, I've learned some disturbing things about her and her past; yes, she has deceived me but who am I to judge her? I've lied on plenty of occasions and have used deception as well to a point where I could have gotten myself killed. I know longer want that type of drama and stress. I know longer want that type of life anymore.

There will come a time when I'll have to tell Jasmine that I have to move on no matter how interested a life with her may seem. My heart truly beats for Olivia and I saw a side to her that I didn't think I would have ever seen when my mother passed away. She was compassionate and cared for me at my weakest moment; for the first time in our relationship I felt safe and could trust her intentions.

This is how I felt when we first started our journey together and now my heart is beating to a different song for her, believe me I'm listening! The night before my mother received her wings, she whispered to me,..."*Son marry that woman.*" She knew something then. She had her own feeling about Olivia and the look she had in her eyes when she gave me her blessings meant the world to me.

I don't know how Olivia feels about this but I've made up my mind and I'm not turning back.

****What Olivia Is Thinking****

I have fallen in love with this man all over again. He has shown me a very vulnerable side of him that I had not known existed. My heart hurts for him because he lost his mother and that part of him could never be replaced.

I wish that I could have felt that way when my father died but I didn't because he made my life such a living hell. I was glad to see him go. I really don't know how I would feel if my mother passed because my feelings for her, even to this day, are still indifferent.

My motivation now is to be happy and live the rest of my days with my King. Our time since we have been back has been absolutely wonderful; we have actually spent every moment with one another. Arguments have ceased and anything that even closely resembles drama has been ignored.

Alexander and Walter has not been a factor. Their presence has not surfaced since our return. I really want to come clean with Kayne about what he doesn't know because I feel that it is just the right thing to do. I really want to release all of my skeletons so they can never come back to haunt me in my happiness, however, the smarter part of my brain doesn't want to mess up the best chemistry me and my man are having at this moment. I want to protect our relationship and keep the harmony.

I want to spend the rest of my life with Kayne and if he doesn't know it I will do my best, every day, to make him feel special and supported. My days of being slick and trying to get over on people are over.

Whether we are rich or poor my desire is to remain with Kayne and faithful to our future together. I fell in love with Jamaica and if we could pick up right now to leave Los Angeles forever I wouldn't hesitate to do so. I felt peace there and I want that feeling on a daily basis no matter what it takes to get there I am be open to it.

It's time to leave all the drama behind me and yes I may be running away from my past but I'm fine with that. Some things are better left in the rear view mirror and I will have to learn to have a short memory.

In the back of my mind I still remember what Walter said and the tape that he has of him having sex with me. He said that if I don't marry Kayne then my secrets would be safe.

As much as I want to marry Kayne, I simply cannot risk Walter telling him about my past, in his desperation to keep us apart. If Kayne and I were to continue our life together and he never asked me to marry him, I would be ok with that until we left to go to a place where we could never be found again.

What Jasmine Is Thinking

Kayne has been very short with me in his responses and I'm not sure what that means. Yes, I told him that I would give him time to make a decision about what he wants to do with his interactions with Olivia but never did I think he would take the liberty, on his own to totally ignore me. I know that his mother just passed away and maybe he is still mourning from his loss and that is understandable but I'm missing him.

My calls go straight to voicemail and my emails are not being returned. I can't take this too much longer. I need to speak with him face to face to see where I stand with him. Being away from him has only made me desire him more; I just can't help myself.

I don't want her to win. I have to have Kayne for myself. If he won't come to me, then I'll go to him. Whatever it's going to take to get Kayne to see that he needs to be with me is what I'm going to do.

I am in love with him and he needs to know just how much. It's time to book a flight to Los Angeles so that I can bring him home where he belongs.

At Walter's House with Alexander

"I don't know what's going on Walter but I haven't seen Olivia or that motherfucking Kayne in a while. I think they have moved from their place and her cell number has changed. She is going to make me look for her again. She is really disrespecting me.

Walter is in his own world, not really paying attention to what Alexander is saying.

"Brother, you know I've been thinking a lot lately and there's an itch that I need to scratch." Alexander doesn't quite understand what Walter means by his statement; Alexander asks for a bit of clarification.

"What exactly are you talking about?" Pulling out a big cigar from his drawer and lighting it; Walter inhales a deep puff from his stogie before he answers. "We have to take care of Kayne. He's the itch I'm talking about and I need to scratch that bitch so he doesn't exist anymore and the closest thing to him is Olivia."

Alexander is still trying to figure out his brother's angle. "What the hell do you mean by bringing up Olivia's name Walter? What does she have to do with this?"

"Let's just say she's the link to a mutual interest. Kayne has some business with me that has to be settled and it needs to be settled fast so do what you have to do to find them; when you do please let me know. This is not a time for you to get personal dammit. You want to find Olivia don't you?" Alexander nods his head yes.

"And I want them both. Kayne soured a business deal of mine and profited from it. I can't let him get away with that."

Alexander didn't ask any more questions and left his brother's house that night with intentions of finding

Olivia. Walter sat at his desk and stared at pictures of him and Regina that he placed in the desk drawers.

The thought of his wife possibly being pregnant from Kayne is just too much for him to accept and if it takes him to go through hell and high water, risking his political status in jeopardy, he will not let Kayne get away with fucking his wife on his dime.

He knew if he got Alexander involved this would turn into a messy fiasco but he didn't care; in his mind, the messier the better. He is counting down the moments until he sees both Kayne and Olivia again, face to face.

Kayne and Olivia's Moments

The summer is almost over and we have truly enjoyed our time together. Money is ok; I managed to save a lot from my excursions, not to mention Olivia has picked up some private catering work that she has become a success.

Life couldn't be better. As we sit at the table enjoying a candlelight dinner that I prepared for her, we engage in conversation.

"Olivia, I want you to know that I have enjoyed my time with you and I want to thank you for all the support that you have given me since my mom passed. I don't know how I could have ever have done it without you; I just wanted to say thank you so much baby. I love you."

We raise our glasses and toast to us and she reaches across the table to give me a kiss.

"You are my man Kayne and it is my duty to be there for you. I knew that you were in pain and I only did what I thought I should have done which was to comfort you in your time of need. I have to admit though; it's kind of ironic that it would be the loss of your mother that brings us closer together. Your mother was a beautiful woman with an even lovelier spirit and sense of humor."

We laugh and start talking about our trip home and the conversations we had with her.

It's a clear night in Los Angeles and the Santa Ana winds are slowly kicking up as they always do in the summer. The sliding glass door is open and in our view, you could see the moon sitting right above the mountains.

I got up to go turn some music on to set the mood. Olivia smiles as I walk by her. I decide to select my Luther Vandross station on Pandora and just let it play. I look at Olivia and summon her to come to meet me in the middle of the living room.

Without hesitation she places her napkin from her lap on the table and pushes away and begins to slowly walk toward me. Willingly, she grabs the napkin from her lap and places it in her plate; methodically, she pushes away from the table and seductively walks toward me.

My seductive gaze communicated my sensual intentions; they must have told her to remove her clothing because with every calculated step, she removed an article of clothing; by the time she reaches me, she is stripped of everything.

I quickly followed suit and joined her. *If This World Was Mine* is playing softly in the background providing a sexy back drop to what I am feeling at the moment. As we slow dance to the music I lovingly rub and caress her ass and softly kiss her lips and neck.

The sounds of heavy breathing fills the room, almost drowns out *Luther's* serenade to our evening; we both know what is about to happen. Candles are adding to the mood of the evening while the light from the full moon, cascading through the patio door, casting a beam of soft light onto the living room floor.

I gently lay Olivia on the Persian rug and begin to passionately suck her toes. This was always a weak spot for her; it made her go crazy. I place every single toe in my mouth and cover them with warm saliva while I take my time attending to each one individually.

I see her eyes rolling back in her head; I can tell that she is cannot handle it and wants me inside her immediately but I refuse to give her wishes just yet, there more to accomplish.

My plan for this Persian rug is far from being complete. I slowly spread her legs and moisten her thighs with my tongue. I lick between them in the direction of her goodies and she grinds her hips forcefully, ready to pounce on me, her prey.

My dick is rock solid and ready to start drilling but I remained poised because I wanted to take her to a place that she had never been before.

"Baby turn over and arch your back and put that ass in the air for me." Moaning and grinding her hips in the air while I spread her ass wide open and begin my analingus performance, using my tongue and lips to give her pleasure.

The motion of my tongue causes her to quiver with excitement; she her head, breaths deeply and receives what I have to offer. Her entire body is squirming, convulsing and trying to take the stimulation. Her muscles become tense; then relax; they tense once more and start then repeat the pattern, again and again.

In a raspy voice she says, "Kayne, let me have you now baby; let me feel you now." I whisper in her ear, "Not yet baby; I'm not ready to give it to you just yet."

By this time in the evening, the moon has shifted its position in the sky, casting brighter glimmers of light upon us as if we were actors on Broadway. The candles have gone out which allows the moonlight to take center stage. After eating her luscious fat ass Olivia pleads with me again, in her most convincing voice.

"Baby can I have you now! My pussy is so fucking wet. It's throbbing for you." I'm ready so I lay on my back with my legs facing the balcony, just enough for the light to cast a soft glow in my direction; Olivia gets up to reposition herself.

"Suck on me first baby, will you do that?" She nods her head yes and starts to suck slowly on my thick head. "Yes baby, don't use your hands and suck it real slow for me…Yeah, baby just like that."

She knows how I like my head and she gives it to me like I want it. 100% no teeth and lots of saliva; she gave me a shine that glistened and lit up the room.

As she starts to get into it and takes more of me in her mouth, I see her pause for a minute and give my dick a second look. I know where head mind is, what she is trying to figure out but I didn't say anything.

She goes back to my head and proceeds to deep throat every inch of my dick to the back of her throat. "Ohhhhhh shit baby yes that feels good, don't stop." She swallows the saliva that has collected in her mouth and goes deep again. As she gives me fellatio, she takes a closer look at what is shining underneath the moonlight between my legs.

She examines the area, pauses and asks, "Kayne, what is this?" I smile as she investigates. She then grabs my balls and sees that there's a black ribbon tied around the base of my dick and balls and something was dangling from it.

"No you didn't!!!!!! This cannot be what I think it is." She gets up, runs and turns on the light and comes back. I quickly close my legs. She returns and slaps my legs open.

"Open your legs Kayne!!"

I politely follow her directions and slowly open them again. Her eyes light up like a child who was opening their most desired Christmas present. I sit up and untie the bow from around my balls and smile from ear to ear because I knew that she wasn't expecting this.

I notice she contains her excitement and begin to tear up because she knows what's about to happen. I purchased a 5 Karat Princess Cut Flawless Diamond engagement ring. While sitting in the middle of our living room floor, naked, I pull her close to me and ask, "Olivia baby, I would like to know if you would be interested in spending the rest of your life with me?"

Tears rolling down her face, she's breathing heavily. She is taking in the moment we just shared and doesn't respond.

So I ask her again. "Baby, I want you to be my wife. I want forever with you and if you say yes you would make me a very happy man." Still no response and tears are washing through her pores. After a few more seconds, she nods her head yes and says, "Yes Kayne…yes I will marry you!!" and I place the ring on her finger.

She gives me a hug and doesn't let me go. We just sit in the middle of the living room naked in the glare of the moonlight basking in the beginning of our initial bliss as we will begin our journey to become man and wife.

CHAPTER 19

THE PLANNING

Kanye's Thoughts

Weeks have passed and we are still in celebrated bliss about our upcoming wedding. We decide that we are not going to prolong this and the wedding would be held at the end of the summer are setting all plans in motion. I have hired the best wedding planner in Los Angeles who specializes in short notice ceremonies.

Olivia has been out with her girlfriends trying on dresses and looking for shoes. She said she wants a private ceremony without all the fluff but I want her to have something special so I decide to go all out for her on her special day.

Olivia didn't have much growing up and she had to fight and claw for what she did receive. I want her to remember this day for the rest of her life so I will spare no expense on seeing her happy. I reach out to some of my buddies and told them I was getting married.

They were all surprise but very happy for me. Unanimously, I was the one they all believed would never settle down and get married and here I am about to do the inevitable. However, what's a little peculiar is that I seem to be more excited about the wedding than Olivia is, she has been pretty calm and not making a big deal out of it which strikes me as odd. Gone are my days of being on the clock; I am happily hanging up my Cocksman ways.

I know that Olivia said she wanted it to be a private affair but there was something I just had to do. If I'm going to make an announcement, I'm going to do it big so I called The Los Angeles Times and paid for a wedding announcement to announce our engagement and upcoming wedding to the entire city.

I had no problem letting my once upon a time clientele know that I would be off the clock forever. I didn't tell this to Olivia and won't until the last minute; I know she will be very surprised that I would go to those lengths to pledge my love and commitment to her. I know my mom is looking down on me and smiling. I have finally reached a point in my life where I'm ready to completely surrender my feelings and let down all of my emotional guards. Olivia has proven to me that she could be my rock. The end of the month cannot come fast enough for me.

****Olivia Is Thinking****

I cannot believe I told Kayne yes that I was going to marry him considering what Walter said to me.

He is so excited; I couldn't look him in the eyes and tell him no or to let's think about it first. I cannot risk the fact that Walter can show up anywhere and fuck my entire life up which is why this has to be a very private affair.

I have been feeling sick to my stomach lately. I don't know if it's my anxiety over what Walter or even Alexander would do if they found out I was about to married or I'm just really nervous about Kayne and I finally being together forever; either way I have to suck it up because I have a wedding to plan.

I wish that I was closer to my mother so that she could help me with this process but our estranged relationship forbids pleasantries at this time so I will have to depend on some of my girls and old co-workers who looked out for me in my earlier days to assist me in the planning process. I pray that Kayne will want to leave Los Angeles and move to Jamaica immediately. That's where I will feel safe and most comfortable. I will try to convince Kayne to do so as soon as we tie the knot. Besides our close friends and family knowing, our marriage will be the best kept secret ever. I guarantee this information will never get out.

Time Does Fly

Its three weeks until our wedding and the planner has done a fantastic job in planning our special day. Olivia has been out all day getting some last minute things done with her friends and I'm at home relaxing and looking at old pictures of my mother. What I would do if I could have her here with me right now. To hear her voice and to take in all of her worldly advice would be priceless. Nevertheless, I will just have to settle for the memories these pictures have captured as well as the thought of knowing that she is in heaven smiling down on us and saying something witty at the same time.

Every morning, I've been hiding our LA Times when it arrives at our door for a reason. The ad that I put out announcing our wedding has been running for weeks now and it has caused uproar from my Cocksman clients. I checked my old email account where I did my business and I received some horrible emails from past clients who would not be getting a piece of me anymore. Who the hell cares though? I'm not about that life any longer and I cannot wait for Olivia to get home so that I can show her so that we can laugh at some of these women who clearly don't want me to be happy.

I have also been ignoring Jasmine's text messages and emails too; I feel bad and I do find myself thinking sometimes about how she makes me feel but I just don't have the history with her despite our past. The honest thing for me to really do is to let her know my choice and not string her along because she has been nothing but honest with me. My fear paralyzes me and I unable to deliver that message to her for two reasons.

I really don't want to disappoint her for one and the other reason is that if I look into her eyes again she may foil all of this wedding talk and I cannot risk becoming vulnerable for her because her eyes are my weakness and the power of her stare breaks me down every time. She has a look that awakes my soul and summons it to her. If I want to stand a real chance at being faithful and happy with Olivia I must remain as far away from Jasmine as possible, nonetheless, I do owe her an explanation on my choice and I will call her the night before the wedding to let her know.

Who knows how she will respond and at this point in time, there's really nothing that I can do about it. Everything has been confirmed and even my brother has made his plans to be in attendance. We decided that there was not going to be a wedding party; just Olivia and me standing in front of our invited friends and family and the pastor who will pronounce us Man and Wife.

August 30th cannot get here fast enough.

I hear keys rattling in the door. I take the current LA Times that I have on the chair and hide it in the sofa before Olivia opens the door.

"Hey baby. How are you?" She comes over and gives me a kiss.

"I'm so tired baby. Look I'm happy to be getting married but this short notice shit that we are doing is taxing!"

She puts her bags down, kicks off her heels and sits next to me on the love seat. "Did you speak to the planner? Is everything set? Did you talk to the pastor? Did you call the caterers for the reception hall? Did you……" as I cut her off in mid-sentence, "Liv, everything has been taken care of baby. All you have to do is show up. I have called everyone on the list you gave me to show up and I've contacted my people too. Everyone is excited for us in anticipation of the big day. You can relax baby."

She reaches over and gives me a hug. When she releases me, I look into her eyes. "Promise me that you will always take care of me like this" and gives me a kiss. "And that's why I love you baby. I'm hungry Kayne, are you cooking?" as she heads to the kitchen to look in the refrigerator.

I take the LA times from the couch and place it next to me. "Baby, I have something I want to show you." Still searching for something to nibble on, she grabs a piece of fruit and brings it with her and sits back on the love seat. "What's up baby?"

I pull out the paper and hand it to her. She looks at it confused; she doesn't know why I have given it to her. I'm smiling at the face she is making because obviously she could care less about reading it. "What am I looking for baby, the sports section?" I shake my head no and say to her, "Go to the local section and tell me what you see."

She turns the pages and goes to the section where we are front page with pictures and details. I sit anxiously to await her screams of happiness. She gets to the local section and her eyes get as big as marbles but she doesn't utter one word. I look at her for a response and she doesn't even look back at me. You could hear mice whispering in the room at that very moment as Olivia just stared at the article. It didn't take long before she starts to breathe heavily and her eyes started to water. Maybe she has a delayed response to the joy of seeing what I had done so I sit and wait to hear what she has to say.

"Kayne!! How long has this ad been running?" I'm still waiting to get that excited response from her I reply, "Close to a month now. I wanted to surprise you with it baby. I wanted to let the city know that this Cocksman was done with that life and I was going to marry the woman I loved. You should see some of the email responses I have already gotten because of it, wait until you see some of them. I can't believe that there are people in the world who don't want to see folks happy. Let me go and get my computer."

I start to get up and Olivia throws down the paper. "You shouldn't have done this! This wasn't necessary Kayne. Why in the fuck did you have to run an ad in the biggest paper in the gotdamn city?!!!!"

Now I'm clueless?! In my mind I'm thinking that this is a good thing and a badge of respect. This was something to show my future wife that I was committed to the rest of our lives together and she is not happy at all about what I thought was a regal gesture.

"What is your problem Olivia? It's just an ad announcing our wedding.

"This was supposed to be private Kayne and here the fucking entire city knows the day, the time and the motherfucking location to where we are going to be married. This was to be a private controlled setting. What happened to that agreement Kayne?"

I'm puzzled at the response I am getting from Olivia. This is some shocking shit to me and there has to be a reason why.

"What is your problem Olivia? I thought this was good." I pick up the paper and look to see if there was a misprint or something or maybe she didn't like the picture I submitted of us.

"Kayne, this wasn't necessary, you had nothing to prove to anybody." While getting up to walk away, she quickly puts her hand over her mouth and runs into the kitchen and throws up in the sink. I follow behind her to check to see what was going on.

"Are you ok Olivia? Damn, I didn't realize that this ad was going to make you so upset that you vomit. I'll call and have them stop running the ad tomorrow. Excuse me for giving a damn" and I walk away to the room leaving her bent over face deep in the sink.

After hearing her bring up all of her insides for the next fifteen minutes she comes into the room.

"Kayne look, I'm sorry. I shouldn't have reacted like that. Will you accept my apology? I just overreacted to something that was trivial but we did say it was going to a small private ceremony and I understand why you wanted to let people know but baby you don't have to worry about proving anything to me. I will take you at your word until you show me different."

I could only appreciate her even more despite the misunderstanding.

"You are right babe. I will call tomorrow and have the ad removed. But how are you feeling? Did you eat something that didn't agree with your stomach or something?"

Olivia goes to the bathroom to clean up a bit but I still have to wonder why she reacted in such a way. I know we said that we would bury our secrets in Jamaica but the look in her eyes told a scary story. I'm not going to press her about it. We are too close to our special day and I want it to go off without a glitch.

More Days Pass….It's The Night Before

It's the night before the wedding and my closest friends have gotten into town. Although I haven't seen some of them in years, I always kept in touch with them. We will remain close forever, in fact are very much like blood brothers.

Matthew was the quiet, slick one. Smooth with a capital 'S' and always says, "I deal in facts." So you know if you got into a heated discussion with him he would cut you with truth and will deliver it so smooth that it would piss you off because it wouldn't be anything you could dispute. Our history goes way back because he is my cousin and we shared many laughs and excursions during our high school days.

Delvon, well he is the friend that I've known since the 2nd grade. His favorite saying is, "I love me some me, if they don't like me, Mother made them and Motherfuck them." The shit sounded funny when he says it because he says it with such conviction and although he may have been the shortest of the crew he had one of the biggest hearts and I appreciated his friendship.

Big Nix was a cool cat. He and I share the same affinity for smoking Cigars and playing golf. Nix thought he was a ladies man too and because he had light brown eyes he always thought that was the Kryptonite to every woman. He would always say, "Let them bitches look into my eyes if they want to, it's a wrap!", always keeps everyone in stitches, cracking up.

And lastly there is Antonio. Antonio is a ladies man in his own mind and thinks he is the Cat's meow. He always referred to himself as, "I'm M.K. bitch!" like who in the hell know what those initials mean. Although a character in his own right, he is a solid dude who I've had many long conversations with about life.

I loved these dudes and they love me as well. There are never any judgments when we got together. It was just pure fun and laughter. I'm glad they made it to see me jump this broom and if time would have permitted, they would have been my groomsman in this wedding but they know and understand and are cool with just being there to share me in my moment. If anything ever went down, these are the guys I would call for help and trust me; there is no limit on how ride or die they would be for me. My brother hasn't made it yet. His flights were delayed but he sent me messages stating that he would be front and center at the church come tomorrow and to not worry. For my bachelor party we decided to fly into Vegas for an overnight turnaround trip.

The things that happened will never be discussed and will go down as monumental. Roosters will always be Red and doors will always be Green. What happens in Vegas…… just happens!!!

Olivia and her girls spent the day in Santa Barbara getting massages, pedicures and going on wine tastings. She text me pictures throughout the day but also tells me she has been throwing up still and says it's all because she is nervous. I didn't think much of it because I knew she was going to be nervous as it got closer to the date.

Tomorrow is our big day and life as I know it is about to drastically change. It will finally be Kayne and Olivia…….Forever.

CHAPTER 20

THAT BITCH

The Big Day Has Arrived

Today is the day that all of the magic happens. I stayed home last night while Olivia spent the night in a hotel in a Suite. It gave us both time to envision the rest of our lives together and everything that we would like to accomplish.

I thought about how over the years we have gone through many trials and tribulations and we seem to have overcome them. Yes, we both have had our shortcomings and trust issues. I feel we will always have those issues but at this point in our lives anything that we keep secret is best for the both of us and needs not be discussed.

I have thrown my judgmental book in the garbage when it comes to Olivia and she has done the same for me. I have enough money saved up so that we could truthfully make a home in the islands and Olivia doesn't know it yet but I have already put money down on some property not far from where my mother was born. I'm excited about what is to come after today and I know when I look into Olivia's eyes and the Pastor asks me do I take her to be my wife; my tears will speak for themselves.

Olivas Dilemma

I woke up feeling like shit today. Yes, I'm nervous and happy and I cannot wait to get this wedding over. I'm still pissed that Kayne chose to announce it to the city. I'm so glad he wanted to show his commitment to me considering his past lifestyle and his intentions of putting everyone on notice but more than just his clients read the LA Times and that concerns me a great deal.

I feel bloated and fat and I'm just not feeling sexy at all and I know I'm going to catch hell trying to get into this dress. My girlfriends will be here shortly to help me get ready. Kayne is so wonderful. He made sure that I had everything in place so that I wouldn't have to do anything for this day. He got the best people to help and although this was a short notice wedding it has gone off without a hitch.

I look forward to spending the rest of my life with this man whom I have loved since the day I walked into his hotel room. I knew that the days of me not having the best had ended when he said hello to me. There's a confidence about him that gives me security and although we have had our insecure and trifling moments, we have fought the good fight which has led to this day.

There is no need to disclose any information or secrets at this point in time because it would definitely do more harm than good. My life has changed and from this point on we will be held accountable for our mistakes that we make.

My stomach still feels nauseated. As I am getting prepared for this day I feel the need to throw up so I quickly run to the bathroom. I must have been knelt over the toilet for a good 5 minutes before I realized that all of this nausea and weight gain may not be coming from being nervous at all.

I run and get my cell phone and call my girlfriend.

"Lisa, have you left to come here yet?" She replies no and asks, "What's up?" "Can you do me a favor and pick me up a pregnancy test."

Silence separated spoken words between us for a few seconds and she responded," Ok, I got you Liv" and hung up the phone.

Hopefully this is not the case but the symptoms point to it being a possibility. Fuck me!!!!!!. I cannot have this right now. Not today, not ever and I say this because of the circumstances that are involved. There's nothing else more important to me in this world of being able to have Kayne's child but as it stands with my unfortunate luck if I am pregnant I will not know if it's Kayne's or Walter's baby.

Kayne and I are very cautious when we decide to make love. He has no problems using condoms. I can count the times that we haven't used them on one hand.

I told Walter to use a gotdamn condom. Maybe I should have risked getting my ass beat and tried running out of there. Maybe I shouldn't have ever gone there in the first place and none of this shit would be a concern on my mind but I knew I had to if I ever stood a fair shot at happiness.

I have to be the dumbest chick on the planet but what was I to do? Walter and Alexander will forever hold my past over my head and that is why I stayed in a fucked up position as long as I did. I was afraid and had no place to go and now I have dug a deeper hole than ever before. I knew it just couldn't be that easy for him. They are foul and they live to ruin people's lives, literally. Twenty minutes have now passed and there's a knock at my hotel door.

I go over and look through the peep hole and notice that it's Lisa. "Heyyyyyyy girl, Are you excited about your wedding day?" "Lisa, I want to be but I got so many things on my mind right now and I just can't focus. Lisa grabs a small bag out of her purse and hands it to me.

"Here is the test you requested. They had a buy one get one free so I got two just in case you will need one for after your honeymoon" and she smiles and winks her eye.

I'm not really amused because I need to know right now if all this nausea is because I'm carrying a child. I take the test and quickly go to the bathroom. I remove it from the packaging and read the instructions. I sit on the toilet so that I could urinate on the stick like it said and I waited. I could hear Lisa asking, "So are you ok Liv? What does it say?"

There has not been a change on the stick yet so I replied, "Nothing yet!" And wait. Then a few seconds later I start to see the blue line appear. It seems like the indicator knew I was very interested in getting the results because it took what seems like forever to decide if it wanted to display a positive or negative sign. After five minutes of waiting the answer was revealed.

"Hey Liv, what does it say? Are you pregnant or not?!!! The suspense is killing me girl!"

I can't believe what I'm seeing so I go back and read the instructions and my heart begins race. I throw the stick in the garbage and I pull the other out of the packaging. I know this must be a fucking mistake, this can't be! I urinate again on the applicator and wait for the results.

I'm pregnant. What in the hell is happening? Why me lord? This can't be fucking happening!!!!!!!

By this time Lisa is knocking on the door. "Liv are you ok?" I quickly grab the first stick from the trash, wrap both sticks in toilet paper, place them back into the bag and hide them away in the bathroom. I wash my hands and open the door with a fake smile on my face.

"It was negative girl. I don't know why I was stressing over that. I have just been nervous about the wedding that it has made me feel kind of sick some days." Lisa looks at me with a smirk on her face. "Well I guess the nervousness also made you eat a little more because yo' ass got some hips now," and we both laugh it off and walk back into the room. "Ok my dear, the makeup artist is on her way. Let's get you ready to look like a princess on your day." And we proceeded to paint the perfect picture of my now tainted future with Kayne. Five more hours to go before I look into my man's eyes and say 'I Do' with a baby in my stomach that may not be his.

*** *The Congressman, Regina and Alexander* ***

"Walter, this shit will not be going down today. There is no way in hell that I will let her do this to me."

Walter still looking at the paper where he sees the ad about the wedding and shakes his head and says, "The balls of this motherfucking Kayne are as huge as a bull."

Walter sees the anger on Alexander's face and shares the same sentiment. He remembers the words that he gave Olivia about this and can't believe she has gone against them. He goes to a safe hidden behind a picture on the wall in his home office and pulls out an envelope which has the zip file of the video. Alexander looks at Walter with interest and concern." What is that you got?"

Walter closes the safe and stares back at Alexander with a sinister look on his face. "The secret that's going to stop this fucking wedding from happening, that's what I got." He walks to the door of his office and calls out to his wife, "Regina, come in here please. "

After a few seconds, a visibly pregnant Regina walks into the room. Alexander looks at her in shock because he didn't realize that she was pregnant.

"Congratulations are in order I see, I didn't know that you were pregnant Regina. Y'all sure can keep a secret." Regina looks at Walter without saying a word to Alexander because she knows that he doesn't have a clue what is going on.

"Yes, she sure can keep a secret alright. Go and put on your Sunday best Regina; we are going to a wedding today."

As Jasmine Reads While In Los Angeles

I have been in Los Angeles for a week without being able to contact Kayne. Why is he ignoring me? What did I say to run him away from the possibility of us being together? I just can't leave without seeing him. I've been in this room bored without his company and I'm missing him. I want to feel his touch again. I want to smell us in the air again. I want Kayne to be mine and if I have to relocate here for now I will.

I go and grab some of the old newspapers that have collected outside of my room door and begin to look in the ads to see how the housing market is in LA.

After searching thru almost all the copies I grabbed the last one to see if I had missed out on previous ads and as I turned the pages I get to the local section and something catches my eye.

I look a little closer and begin to read the advertisement. After a few minutes of allowing the information to sink into my head I just start crying uncontrollably. I couldn't believe what I was reading. This is why he wasn't responding to my calls and text. Why couldn't he just tell me? Why would he just leave me out in the cold like this? What is it about her that he loves so much when he knows that I'm better for him? I go back to reading the ad and see that their wedding is today. There is no way I'm missing this. He is going to have to look me in the eye and make me believe that marrying her is what he really wants to do. I quickly get up and go to the bathroom to get ready. My heart is hurting. This just cannot be happening!

On The Way To The Church

All dressed and ready to go. I'm in the limo headed toward the church. I decide that I didn't want anyone else with me during this moment of clarity as my past is running through my head. From the days of my childhood that shaped me to be the man I am today to the loss of my mother and why Jah had to take her away before she was able to witness me get married. I know she is still with me though. I can feel her presence.

But there's still the thought of Jasmine on my mind. I said to myself that I would call her the night before but I just couldn't do it. I'm sure I could have handled this differently with her but I just couldn't look her in the face again to deliver my decision. I know I have to call her because it's just the right thing to do and she deserves to be treated better than this.

I pull out my cell, scroll to her name and press call. A part of me was hoping that she would ignore my call and just send me to her voicemail because I really wasn't prepared to let her in on what was about to happen in my life. After four rings, there is still no answer and her voicemail picks up. I pause for a minute to gather my thoughts and words before I speak. "Hello Jasmine, this is Kayne and I hate that I have to make this phone call and leave you this message like this but this was the only way I felt that I could do it. I just couldn't look into your eyes and tell you face to face." I take a deep breath and I finish my message. "I have decided to marry Olivia……..today. I'm sorry Jasmine." And I press end to finish the call.

I can't believe that I just made that call and left her that message. That was probably one of the hardest decisions I ever had to make. Thoughts of forever with Jasmine will always be a thought in my mind but the reality of that possibility was just washed away when I decided to leave her that message. All I could do was look out of the window of the limo and stare at the happy people as I passed them by on my way to my future Olivia.

It's Time To Get Married

I'm in the waiting room of the church all alone. My buddies have just left after playfully giving me shit about this big ass mistake I'm about to make. There is always laughter when we get together and today was no different. As I sit back and close my eyes while waiting for the ushers to retrieve me from my room there's a knock on the door. I go to open it and see that it's my brother. He made it! We just gave each other a bear hug and cherished that moment. "You made it bruddah!!!!!!! Damn it's so good to see you again." He comes in and sits down. "Kayne, it's good to see you again. Man, I can't believe you are about to tie the knot? Are you ready? "I look at him and laugh, "Hell No I'm not ready but I'm going to do it anyways!" And we both fall out in laughter. Time is getting near now and my bro and I have had a good quick conversation where we discussed everything. Before he leaves the room he turns to me and says, "Muddah would be so proud of you Kayne. She is here watching today. Make her proud. I love you bruddah." And he exits the rooms leaving me there with water in my eyes feeling a million different emotions.

Not too long after my brother leaves, the usher knocks on my door. "It's time for the ceremony." I say a prayer before I walk out and kiss the sky in hopes that my Muddah receives my Love.

At The Alter

Well here we are. The day has finally come when we will become man and wife. As I look out into this church, I can see my family and friends smiling, filled with happiness for me. I can also see that some of Olivia's friends and old co-workers are in attendance too.

I know that some of these folks here are surprised to be witnessing this because this was a moment that I never expected for myself and I couldn't be any happier. As I stand here attempting to hide my nervousness I also see the back doors of the church opening and there she is….MY BRIDE.

I can already see from a distance that her face is full of tears as she is walking down the aisle to get to me.

She passes each pew with slow and calculated steps toward her King.

From Olivia's P.O.V.

As I take my time to proceed down this long aisle I take a quick glimpse to see all who have attended today. The church was decorated beautifully and there were more people there than I expected. My friends and old co-workers are there in support and they're smiling at me as I'm walk down towards Kayne. Then suddenly I hear a voice calls out my name very quietly. I look over and see that it's Walter. Ohhhhh My God!!!!!!!! He is here at my wedding!!!! I knew something like this was going to happen. It took everything in me not to scream and just run away then but I kept my poise. He holds up a zip file and he winks at me. I also see that Regina and Alexander are there too. DAMN!! In my head I say a prayer to God and continue toward the alter to Kayne. "God, please give me the strength to make the right decision today. I beg you."

Kayne's P.O.V.

As I'm staring at my Queen, I realize that she is what beauty only wishes it could be. I could not wait to hear her say *"I DO"* because finally I was secure with me and my choice to take her to be my lawfully wedded wife.

I erased all of my inhibitions about Love and I am ready to make a home with Liv. I am no longer interested in the Cocksman lifestyle. I want to have real Love like my parents had. I want the responsibility of sharing happiness with her.

She reaches the end of the aisle, takes my hand and looks me in the eyes. They were bloodshot red and full of tears. I leaned over and whispered to her, "I Love you baby." Understanding the emotions that are overcoming the both of us I can truly appreciate what she is going through as I have allowed my tears to flow freely gathering in a puddle of happiness in what she and I are about to share.

I made it momma!!!

Love has found me again!!!! My heart has healed from the scars and I'm ready to give it to my Queen on this day for safe keepings.

The pastor begins the ceremony while the guests watch in awe. I look into the crowd and all I could see was my brother smiling back at me. I guess the ad that I put in the paper brought out more people than I would have imagined but so what, this is a happy time for me and the more witnesses the merrier.

The pastor goes on and speaks about how when a man finds a wife he finds a good thing as he is preaching a good sermon today. The time has come when he ask me, "Do I take Olivia to be my wife?" Loudly and proudly I respond, "I DO!" He now looks to Olivia and ask her the same question.

"Do you take Kayne to be your lawfully wedded husband for the rest of your life Olivia?" She looks into my eyes and I smile at her hoping that it would ease her nervousness but she doesn't respond. Maybe her nerves have finally gotten the best of her; she is at a loss of words. So the pastor asks her again jokingly as the guest's laughter echo in the church but she doesn't crack a smile.

Now my smile turns to concern because her face is showing pain and anguish, the tears that flow from her eyes are as big as marbles and she is visibly trembling. She turns to the guest and stares in the crowd not blinking an eye and then back to the pastor. And then she sets her eyes back on me; I knew something was definitely wrong. I could hear the guest murmuring amongst themselves because what was supposed to be a happy occasion is now turning out to be very weird. I knew Olivia was about to say something because her lips begin to quiver from nervousness. She grabbed my hand and something deep down inside warned me that this was going to be a moment of clarity. She takes a deep breath and says,

"Kayne, I can't marry you." The guests' gasps in unison. She continues, "Not now; not ever. I'm so sorry!!!" And she turns and runs toward the door to leave the church. Lisa and the rest of the girls quickly get up to follow her. I'm standing at the altar stunned, embarrassed, hurt and confused. I'm in total shock because I can't believe what has just happened to me.

Immediately, I notice a gentleman stand up and runs after Olivia. I found this very odd that someone would do this and as I focused in, I noticed the man who was leaving the church was Alexander. This motherfucker was here at our wedding!!!!!!

It's all making sense to me now. This is why Olivia was angry about the ad I took out. She didn't want to risk the chance of him finding out and ruining our day. Now I feel like shit and I'm angry at the same time. How could I be so stupid!!!

As guests are starting to clamor around in a confused state of mind, I start walking toward the entrance of the church to see if I could find Olivia. As I get halfway down the aisle I notice another man and woman stand up; he begins to clap and smile at me in front of the entire crowd.

Please wake me because this has to be a motherfucking dream that has turned into a nightmare. I knew this was too good to be true. I knew that someway somehow Karma would rear her ugly head again in my life.

It is Walter. He approaches me with a visibly pregnant Regina and whispers to me, "Checkmate motherfucker!" and he walks out of the church doors laughing like someone had just told the funniest joke.

My brother and my boys rush to me to make sure I was OK. I try and hold myself together but I just couldn't because this day has been marred with anguish. I don't know what happened and why Olivia decided to walk out on me but I believe that Walter and Alexander had something to do with it.

I look into my boys' eyes; they visibly look concerned but they do not say a word. My brother comes over to me and says, "You don't have to answer me right now but whatever just happened I don't like at all and somebody will have to pay for this."

I did not want this to happen. One of the reasons why my brother was away was because of some trouble he had gotten himself into and he was no stranger to violence. He was very protective when it came to me.

I find the strength to walk out of the church with my brother and friends beside me and we leave the shocked guest behind. Once we got outside, there was no sign of Olivia, Alexander or Walter. As the guest starts to leave and pass me by, I noticed another familiar face that was also in the crowd that had just witnessed this debacle.

It was Jasmine. She comes up to me with her eyes full of tears and says, "I got the message that you left today Kayne. Thanks for letting me know ahead of time. So this is how you wanted me to find out about "our" forever?" I had nothing to say to her that would make any sense so I just remained quiet and stood there looking stupid as shit. She stares back at me, shakes her head and walks away. I knew that I had hurt Jasmine and there was nothing that I could do now to soften this blow. I had probably just lost the best thing that could have ever come into my life and it was entirely fault.

My sadness has quickly turned to anger because I still can't believe what has just taken place. I tried to be the good guy. I tried to change for the better but the more I try the more I realize I am who I am and that isn't going to change. My past just will not allow me to smile again and be fucking happy. I don't deserve happiness and Karma is making sure that we never meet.

If Alexander and Walter think that they have gotten away with destroying my life, they have another thing coming. They will pay for this shit and as I looked into each one of my boy's eyes they knew what it meant and what is going to have to be done about it. My brother has the same look too and that is not good for anyone involved.

I will spend all of my money and time getting everyone back who was involved in my embarrassment today. Their lives will never be the same. Just like they decided to ruin mine, I will return the fucking favor. They will clearly understand that when they see my ass again it will not be a pleasant encounter. Walter, Alexander and Olivia will feel my wrath and they will soon be reminded that……..

I'M STILL KAYNE MOTHERFUCKER and Revenge is a BITCH!!

Thanks from the Author

I would like to personally THANK all of you who have SUPPORTED me throughout the years. Without your constant belief in me it would be impossible for ANY of this to happen. I fully UNDERSTAND where ALL of my BLESSINGS flow from but without YOU ALL as the participants, my voice would be difficult to hear. I want you to know that not only do I sincerely APPRECIATE you…I also RESPECT that you think enough about my

Work and Career that you will spend your TIME and HARD EARNED dollars to keep MY DREAM ALIVE and RELEVANT. From writing Novels to my Inspirational Books, I have had the pleasure to be re-introduced to the world and gain more SUPPORTERS that have followed me since I started in the industry over 20 years ago. THANK you for the Thousands of emails...The Facebook messages....The Tweets and the HUGS when we meet at the Book Signings. I will continue to provide great work for you to enjoy.

If you haven't purchased

C.O.T.C.-Kayne Revealed Vol.1 or Kayneisms of Inspiration Vol.1

Please go and do so and spread the word. They can be purchased on Amazon.com, Createspace.com and Barnes & Noble in Digital and Paperback.

Continued BLESSINGS, LOVE and SUCCESS to ALL of you.

Sincerely,

OMEGA KAYNE

•Make sure you leave a REVIEW on AMAZON

C.O.T.C.-THE REVENGE IS UP NEXT!!!!

Made in the USA
Columbia, SC
25 March 2020